Amin is a novelist, and a pharmacist living in Calgary, Canada. He has been interested in spiritual upliftment and has studied extensively a Sufi order; thus, he has undertaken to write a work of fiction, *The English Priest*. It is a novel that straddles the world of war with the weakening of the human soul. Redemption is not possible if involved in war, corruption, and greed. Thus, you can see by reading the script, how man is further from uplifting oneself from such an abyss. Through the uplifting of the soul, one can go from the lowest to the highest spiritual accomplishment. This is such a story.

To my family and friends who have encouraged me to write this book.

Amin Karim

The English Priest

Austin Macauley Publishers™
London • Cambridge • New York • Sharjah

This is a work of fiction. Names, characters, businesses, places, events, locales, and incidents are either the products of the author's imagination or used in a fictitious manner. Any resemblance to actual persons, living or dead, or actual events is purely coincidental.

Ordering Information
Quantity sales: Special discounts are available on quantity purchases by corporations, associations, and others. For details, contact the publisher at the address below.

Publisher's Cataloging-in-Publication data
Karim, Amin
The English Priest

ISBN 9781638292050 (Paperback)
ISBN 9781638292067 (ePub e-book)

Library of Congress Control Number: 2023916610

www.austinmacauley.com/us

First Published 2023
Austin Macauley Publishers LLC
40 Wall Street, 33rd Floor, Suite 3302
New York, NY 10005
USA

mail-usa@austinmacauley.com
+1 (646) 5125767

I like to thank my family for their support and patience.
Maulana Rumi and the whirling dervishes of Konya.

Prologue

The path you follow is a river—a river of life.

This journey will require a raft made out of planks of goodwill, tied with ropes of truth. While slowed down by eddies of unfolding history and boulders of obstructionist men, you must depend on a paddle of gentle persuasion and single-minded doggedness. Hope will be your guiding star. Anticipating danger will be impossible as it stares you in your face, threatening your livelihood and your very life. However, like a river, you should persevere, more like propel forward, until you succeed in overcoming all obstacles. Refusing to be silenced by brute force, you will be the human conscience, uprooting corruption and greed wherever and whenever you come across it, because it harms the soul, resulting in misery and despair. The cornerstone of civilized behavior is goodwill, human decency, and respect for others. With such an attitude, you will see the light of HIS creation in all of mankind, and for your work in liberating a soul from its dilemma, aligning it with a trajectory of righteousness, you will earn a place in the divine garden, a Garden of Bliss, where all who believe like you do and are guided by the universal truth will find a well-deserved resting place. This is your reward at the end of the journey.

1
Egypt 1939

If we come to [a state of] anger and battle,
it is a reflection of His Wrath.
And if we come to [a state of] peace and pardon,
it is the reflection of His Love.
– Rumi

Flight BAC 857 took off from London on time. It was September 1, 1939. The pilot announced the devastating news over the intercom:

"Germany has invaded Poland. A large number of roads and bridges have been destroyed. There are hundreds and thousands of refugees on the road. The German air force has destroyed most of Poland's aircrafts, still sitting on the runway."

Wearing a black tunic with a white collar, a willowy and bespectacled man was assigned to seat 14A. Next to him sat a smartly dressed man, clean shaven except for a bushy mustache. A whiff of aftershave floated across the cabin. He stuck out his thick hand.

"Major Ross. Well, we are now at war whether we like it or not," he said, introducing himself.

"Reverend John Wilson, chaplain for the army base at Helwan and the parish of Giza and Al-Fayoum."

"Ah! We have a priest on board," declared Major Ross. "You will pray for a safe flight, won't you?"

"Of course. Not time yet to leave this good earth," the reverend answered confidently. "We have battles to win and enemies to subjugate. Not time yet," John muttered this time to himself, his voice drowned by the engine noise.

As the plane gained momentum on the expansive runway, the two gentlemen discussed the war and colonies. At one point during the conversation, they got animated. The debate drew the eyes of several passengers until they noticed subtle stares around them.

"We need to control ourselves and keep our voices down," the reverend finally advised. "The others are giving us a nasty stare. It is our war, you know, and we have no right to involve the Egyptians or anybody else not connected with the war. Moreover, our enslavement of other races in the name of colonization does not go down too well with the locals, and our looting of their cultural treasures is unethical. No wonder the intelligentsia of these countries is supporting the Nazis just to get rid of us!"

"Well, you know, we have a treaty with Egypt to protect the Suez Canal, to keep it open for traffic, and to ensure that the sea lanes to the East are kept open," the major rebutted. "Our whole empire depends on us keeping Egypt from falling into German hands."

"Egypt has declared itself neutral in this war, and therefore the Germans have no reason to attack it."

"What makes you so sure?" asked the major. "They have attacked most of their neighbors in Europe and occupied them in more or less twenty-four hours. Moreover, it may not be Egypt per se they are after, but the Suez Canal. Once they control the canal, they choke our trade with the Far East."

"Then why don't you make an effort to treat the local population with dignity and protect their cultural treasure from looters?" asked the reverend.

The major's response was swallowed up in the engine noise.

As the reverberating grind of propellers muted their voices, they surrendered conversation and decided to read—the reverend his Bible and the major his maps of the Libyan Desert. The stewardess came around shortly after takeoff offering drinks and snacks.

"Coffee?" she asked.

"With cream and sugar," replied the reverend.

"What about you, sir?" She offered the major.

"Black. Just like the clouds forming outside. The clouds of war," the major added dramatically.

"Shame we had to come to war—it is so mindless," the stewardess replied.

"Mindless, but necessary," the major concluded.

"You see, Reverend," injected the Major, taking a sip of coffee, "the Germans will attack us from here, pointing to an area near Benghazi, in Libya. Then they will try and encircle us here, pointing to an area south of Benghazi."

"I don't have a clue as to the stationing of German or Allied Forces," admitted the reverend. "All I fear is that the war will spill into Egypt with its large urban population centers, and then we will not be able to contain the unfolding of the human catastrophe. Including killing and maiming of innocent civilians. The most affected, the most vulnerable, would of course be women and children."

The heat of the argument rose as each defended his position. The reverend wiped several beads of sweat from his forehead as he pressed on. "Do not forget, we occupied Egypt in 1882, having crushed their nationalist revolt led by Ahmed Urabi, who wanted all Europeans and the Ottoman Turks out of Egypt." The reverend's face reddened with anger. "Occupying other people's land and grabbing their resources is thievery."

"I don't know anything about Egypt's occupation," said the major, "but that happened a long time ago. Protection could be offered if they didn't want self-rule," explained the major. "Self-rule would mean they could tear up the treaty on the Suez Canal and hand over the canal to the Germans."

"They are not likely to do that," responded John. "They need revenue from the canal and for that reason would allow ships to pass through. As for handing it over to the Germans, if we were to treat them fairly, we surely would be better respected and therefore they would have no reason to be bosom buddies with the Germans."

A voice over the loudspeaker announced their ascent, breaking up the conversation. As the plane soared upward, John leaned back in his seat and closed his eyes, thinking about the time he spent at the home office to renew his passport.

"Good morning, Reverend," Nigel greeted.

"Good morning," replied John.

"So, what brings you here?" asked Nigel.

"Visa for Egypt," replied John.

"For how long?"

"Well, for now six months, but you never know—it may take longer to unshackle the soul from greed and corruption," John answered apprehensively.

"I know," replied Nigel. "Difficult to tell right now. You can always renew the visa at the consulate office."

"Yes, of course," said the reverend, handing his passport to Nigel.

Nigel was in charge of intelligence, along with his duties issuing passports to those traveling to the war zone. Major Ross, a fourth-generation soldier, was seconded to the passport office as assistant to Nigel.

"You will be safe if we can arrange the flight for you," Nigel assured.

"That would be nice to know," replied John.

"There is a flight next week," Nigel offered. "Shall I put you on that flight?"

"That would be dandy."

The week couldn't have flown by fast enough as the departure date soon arrived.

"Oh, by the way, Nigel told me that you would be traveling to Egypt," the major interrupted as John's eyes batted open. "You do have an Egyptian childhood friend, don't you? What's his name? Uh…uh, Mustapha, isn't it?"

"Yes, I do," John replied. "I don't know where he is now. I have been away for more than ten years and the last time I heard of him was that he was somewhere in Cairo where he has an uncle. How does Nigel know him?"

"Well, let's just say we have our sources," said the major cryptically. "I believe that he is involved in some anti-British activities and therefore we have restricted his group's places of worship. Anyway, I am glad we are on the same flight."

As the major's word floated around in his head, Reverend John Wilson suddenly grew suspicious. He hadn't expected a passport personal making the flight arrangements for him to inform the military about a pacifist priest traveling on a commercial flight full of soldiers. Yet information, however trivial, was always shared with the military intelligence. John remembered that from his parents, who were sent by the British Museum while the intelligence unit knew everything about their work, their associates, and their discoveries.

John's parents were archeologists excavating a site near Giza where Sumerian clay tablets were discovered. Mustapha's father had helped with the excavation work. John and Mustapha become good friends, playing and learning together. However, there was something unusual about Mustapha. He possessed a keen instinct regarding major events well before they happened. During the excavation work, it was Mustapha who told John's parents where to dig in order to find buried archeological treasures of Babylon.

Among the clay tablets that had come from Ur in Mesopotamia were some drawings on papyrus depicting a wheel with both size and weight scribbled on it. An urban legend existed stating that the Egyptians hid spies in Ur and that the detailed drawings of the wheel were smuggled out of Ur to Egypt. The smuggling was cleverly accomplished. The spies made a small incision on the side of a camel, put the papyrus under its skin, and stitched it back. Various other discoveries, including a clay tablet letter addressed to the local vizier, led to the conclusion that the drawings were smuggled out of Ur, thus giving rise to the brilliant Egyptian civilization around 2900 BC. These clay tablets and the papyrus drawings that lay buried for thousands of years were now shipped through Cairo onto London, where they were sold through local antiques dealers. It was John's mother who mentioned to his father about the missing clay tablets and papyrus drawings that were destined for the Cairo Museum but ended up in London. However, his father did not pay much attention to this. As long as the grant money was coming from the British Museum, he did not care where the tablets or the papyrus ended up.

John realized that his every move was watched and every word spoken was made a note of; therefore, he decided to keep his opinions to himself. He was living in a farcical democracy where the official line was freedom of expression, but privately it was "watch what you say—we are listening and making notes." This hypocrisy was meant for the naïve to swallow as fed by the controlled media, then marketed to the rest of the world as a democracy that believed in "free speech." The state expected its citizens to comply with its "official thinking" while promoting free speech to the outside world.

Pulling a handkerchief from his pocket, John dabbed at his face. It was stiflingly hot in the plane. Moreover, salty sweat intertwined with a pungent smell of beer, making John nauseated. Soldiers were feeling the heat too. Some had removed their heavy khaki shirts and were stripped from the waist up. The major revealed beads of sweat running down his face, which he wiped from time to time with the back of his hand. The stench kept the reverend awake for most of the flight, along with some choice conversation. Racial slurs and profanities flowed like a keg at a party. The reverend ashamedly blushed at what he heard.

"For Christ's sake, stop!" John screamed at the troops when the language simply couldn't get much worse. Turning to Major Ross, he added calmly, "Someone better keep control of your boys. It is unnecessary to toss around racial slurs and profanities. We are using their territory to conduct our war. It seems to me we don't treat humanity with respect. It is our arrogant self again coming to the forefront."

"Boys will be boys, like the saying goes," the major replied, waving off the reverend's request.

"We seem to have immature boys," retorted the reverend.

Silence separated the two men.

A thought of death and destruction hung heavy on John's mind. Peace was like a distant memory—long forgotten and seemingly eons ago. He was among the warriors of a nation and wondered how many of the Europeans tribes would go into battle, filled with hate and revenge, to punish the German aggressors. Wherever he turned there were men in uniform. Nevertheless, there was an exception. Two portly men sitting at the back of the cabin, one dressed in short sleeved blue striped shirt and khaki pants while the other was wearing a khaki shirt and pants. They aggressively fanned their faces with a *The Times of London* newspaper.

"Who are those two men sitting at the back?" asked the reverend.

"Journalists from *The Times of London* sent to cover the war," the major replied.

The rest of the flight was somewhat uneventful. The reverend and the major said little, since the major was asleep most of the time and the reverend busied himself reading the Bible. The flight was long and bumpy. The heavy noise of the engine and the constant chatter of the passengers made the cabin sound like an overworked factory. Accompanying the excessive babble were the snores of the major and a few others on the plane. The sounds of wheezing mixed unpleasantly with the military songs and the unruly behavior of men with alcohol added to their bloodstream.

The reverend could only sleep for a few hours at a time, restlessly tossing and turning. The major ended up asleep on John's shoulder. He gently pushed the major's head off his shoulder. This made the major wake up.

"I am so sorry," he said. "I am a terrible sleeper on flights; you will have to excuse me."

"No harm done," John replied.

The flight was fairly smooth, except when passing over the Mediterranean. The plane began to roll and pitch and the thumping sound of loose baggage in the overhead bins signified that it had not been properly secured. Personal belongings flew all over the place. One soldier was grazed by a razor blade, which left a two-inch gash on his right cheek. Another was hit by a toothbrush, while a third soldier ducked from an oncoming bar of soap. The reverend's Bible landed in his face, then plopped on top of his lap. He picked it up and turned it over. It was open to the gospel of Mark (15.10-20):

"It is what comes out of a person that makes him unclean. For from the inside, from a person's heart, comes the evil ideas which lead him to do immoral things, to rob, kill, commit adultery, greed, and do all sorts of evil things."

He showed the passage to the major, pointing to the words "kill" and "greed."

"Well, isn't war a killing machine and colonies as part of our greed?" asked the reverend. "They are connected, aren't they? Don't you see that? According to Rumi, the great Persian poet, war is God's wrath on man due to greed. Moreover, the Bible condemns greed."

"There are men who believe in the Bible as the gospel truth, while others look at it as a historical document, open to interpretation," retorted the major.

"The end is near," the reverend muttered to himself. "The nightingale will sing soon."

"You said something, Reverend?" asked the major.

"No, nothing. Just talking to myself," and he continued to read.

Hours passed before a jarring thud indicated the plane hit the runway. A wave of relief passed over the passengers as they knew they had arrived. A cheerful roar bounced throughout the cabin as they sang "God Save the King," waking drowsy passengers from their rest. It dawned on John that having sung the national anthem for twenty odd years, if God could only save the king and all else perish, he would be miserable without any subjects left to rule over. Trying to figure this out was too complicated and he wasted no time over it.

The ruckus continued until the plane came to a complete stop. Opening the window shade, John saw that a cloud of sand had blocked the sun out. He looked around and saw terror in the eyes of young soldiers, some as young as fifteen and sixteen, as they sat motionless in apprehension and fear. The temporary numbing of the senses from alcohol had been replaced with the realization that they were in a war zone. Though the plane stood still, there was no great rush for the exit. The reverend was the first to embark through the exit doors. The sergeant major commanded the attention of his soldiers.

"Right, all of you out!" he yelled. "We need to get to the front lines *pronto*."

The harshness of the major's voice terrified the reverend.

The rush for the exit was now on. Mannerisms and politeness took a break while the youthful exuberance of the soldiers overcame the instinct to tremble. A cloud of sand had settled down by now and the rays of blinding sun came through the window. Having spent his childhood in this part of the world, the blazing desert sun still got to John. Each time he came back for a vacation, which was once or twice a year, it took a while before he got used to the heat and the glare.

The doors of the airplane now flung open, a hot blast of desert air rushed in, and a spray of fine sand hit John's face. By the time he reached the bottom of the rickety steps, a bucketful of sand had invaded his nose, ears, and eyes. Rubbing his eyes to remove the sand was a fruitless task. He therefore ignored it, hoping to get used to it. The annoyance of sand in his throat persisted, leaving it raw and raspy. He tried to swallow some saliva, but to no avail.

The airport was a staging area military aircraft used for the war in the western desert. Mechanics in khaki uniforms were busy repairing engines, while spitfires and hurricanes took off and landed in rapid succession.

"Are these hurricanes useful against the Stukas?" John asked a passing mechanic.

"Hurricanes are extremely useful in the desert. They can be used for reconnaissance, patrolling, attacking, and bombing."

Awestruck by the magnitude of the machinery, John continued toward the terminal building. The sickly smell of sweat and beer from the plane was replaced by the pungent smell of a metropolis. A hand tapped John's shoulder and he turned around.

"You must be Reverend John," the man said, shaking John's hand with military force. "I am George, your chauffeur for the day. The ambassador is expecting you for dinner this evening. After you've had a chance to freshen up, I will pick you up from your hotel at six o'clock and take you for supper at the ambassador's house."

"How did he know I was coming?" inquired the reverend.

"All important newcomers to Egypt are invited to the ambassador's residence," George explained. "Besides, the foreign office sent a telegram saying you were coming and that the ambassador should make life easy for you. You being the reverend, it is all the more important that the ambassador meets with you and discusses your needs while you are here in Egypt."

George carefully squeezed the luggage in the trunk and took off at great speed, as if transporting a prisoner from the courthouse to jail. Nearly running over a pedestrian, who cursed him vehemently, George drove through the narrow winding streets, his hand pressed against the horn, the sound of which gave John a headache. Men and beast scattered to the sidewalk. The place had mushroomed out of all recognition. The description provided by Gunner L. E. Tutt provided was authentic:

"It bombards the eyes, the ears, the nose and the nerve endings with a plethora of experiences, all of them new, all of them exciting and stimulating...It is a noisy city, but why whisper when you can shout...trams clang and clatter, their conductors blowing a little pipsqueaks of hunting horns. From every café comes the clatter of backgammon pieces, the gurgle of water pipe and in the background the nasal, off pitch singing from a radio."

There were more people on the streets than he had expected and there was constant jostling for space between the army vehicles, taxis, private cars, trucks, animals, and humans littering the narrow street. The whole atmosphere was one of organized chaos. Although the windows were closed, John could not talk with George. The noise of the car mingled with the deafening canopy of clatter from the streets made any conversation impossible. Not to mention, John's throat was getting worse. He coughed to clear it, encouraging a yellow gluey mass to emerge. He opened his window to expel it and it landed on some poor animal. The animal continued regardless.

John sat quietly, admiring the chaos; occasionally he would sit up when he saw a familiar sight. He reached his hotel in forty minutes. The Desert Inn was located in the suburb of Dokki. As he stepped out of the car, John noticed a few shops and restaurants on either side and across from his hotel. A few houses down, a mosque's loudspeaker dangled loosely from the minaret. A muezzin voice, summoning the faithful to midday prayers, floated out of the loudspeaker like smoke from a chimney. It was the intersection of Tahrir Street and Sudan Street and a few people were praying in the street, concentrating on the divine word, oblivious to the hustle and bustle around them. The power of concentrated prayer was such as to block all outside sounds and distractions. It would be as if they were wearing earmuffs that allowed only the divine word to enter at the expense of all others.

The porter took care of the luggage. As John entered the lobby of the hotel, he noticed a colorful rug lining the floor, a crystal glass chandelier, and a large lazily moving fan hung overhead. A young Egyptian man with a fez cap greeted him.

"I am Omar, and I will be at your service while you are here with us. Please do not hesitate to ask if I can be of any help." It appeared to John that he had a strange look on his face, a look that would be described as hostile. Omar continued, "We have a room ready for you and the bathtub is filled with water, so freshen up and I hope you enjoy your stay here." The last part "enjoy your stay here" was said with a genuine disinterest.

"Thank you. I am sure I will," the reverend replied. The porter picked up John's luggage while John picked up the hand luggage and made their way to room 121 on the first floor. Having climbed a few steps to the first floor, the third room on their left was John's room. As the porter opened the door, John peeked inside. The room was a fair size with one bed, an attached bathroom, and a writing table with some loose paper and a pen. In the far corner was a locked drinks cabinet. The fan hummed softly as it spun and window shutters were closed to keep the heat out. A cool breeze touched John's skin and gave him much-needed relief from the heat. The journey from London had left him dehydrated as he gulped down two glasses of cool water from a jug sitting next to his bed. He then took off his shoes, slumped onto his bed, and soon fell asleep.

In the meantime, downstairs Omar answered an incoming call.

"Ross, here," said the voice at the other end.

"Omar. He has arrived."

"Keep an eye on him, and report any strange comings and goings," Ross demanded as he hung up.

After about an hour of sound sleep, a sharp knock on his door awakened the reverend.

"Sir, the car is here to pick you up," announced a voice. It was the porter.

"It will be a few minutes," John answered, hurriedly jumping out of bed.

He threw open the shutters to let some light in and, although it was evening and despite the fact that his room was facing a courtyard, it was still bright outside. The courtyard had a fountain in the middle surrounded by lush green foliage and flowering shrubs of hyacinth and jasmine. A sweet smell of jasmine wandered across the courtyard and entered John's room. Undressing himself, John plunged into the tepid bath waters. After fifteen minutes, having had his bath, John dried himself with a towel, changed into a set of evening clothes consisting of a loose white shirt and cream-colored pants. Looking at his watch, he realized he was running late and hurriedly made his way downstairs to the lobby. Omar was attending to the newly arrived guests, so he did not bother to speak to him. John looked out of the main doors and noticed a car waiting for him. He knew it was George's, since it was the same car that brought him from the airport. He ran to the car and clamored into the backseat.

"Hello, George. Sorry to have kept you waiting. I must have gotten into a deep sleep," John apologized.

"Not to worry," said George. "We are a little late, but we will make it in time."

Racing down Sudan Street, into Abd El Salam and on to Aref Street, George made a right turn into Gamaat and then into Salem Salah.

"Oh, by the way," George injected into the comfortable silence, "most of the British officers are staying at the Shepherd hotel. We will go there one evening just for a relaxing drink. You may want to meet some of the officers who are running this war."

"And why would I want to meet them?"

"In case the war extends into Egypt and we have to get out fast, a few friends in high places will help."

"God will take care of us when the time comes," John pledged.

As they drove on, a few landmarks became familiar to John. The Aqueduct wall, the Church of St. Barbara, the

Church of Abu Serga, the Ibn Tulun mosque and the Al Azhar mosque. Other sites familiar to him were the Citadel and Hasan mosques. His eyes wandered across each of these landmarks. But it was only at the church of St. Barbara that he somehow could see through its outer wall into the church. He observed a lone woman worshiper in her mid-thirties sitting in the pew. She wore a black outfit with a head covering and she turned and smiled at John. He smiled back. George turned around and looked back at John and he, too, was smiling. John began to wonder what the meaning of all this was.

"Is there something that you know that I don't?" asked John. "I could see through the church wall and I know you could too. That woman? Who is she? It seems to me she looked at me and smiled and she looked at you too. Is there something common between us that I fail to understand?"

George simply smiled. John did not know what to make of it.

"Well, this is how it all fits in," George began. "We were together a long time ago, in fact, when the church was first built centuries ago. You conducted the first service. I was the altar boy and that woman was the first to arrive in the church on that day. The three of us then went our separate ways. The woman you saw there still lives in the church, but as a spirit. She is a guardian angel of the church. You and I have taken birth many times over. We have not been liberated from our earthly bodies. This age is called the *kali yug*, or the Dark Age, where divine knowledge and wisdom in the world are at their lowest level; only a few that acquire it will be saved."

"Can't we stop and see the church?" asked John.

"We are running late for dinner; perhaps another time," said George. "Now tell me, which part of the city is most familiar to you? You came here often from Giza, didn't you?"

"Not that often, maybe once or twice a year."

"The city has grown a lot; it is the people from the countryside who have come into the city and created all the traffic chaos we have," George elaborated.

"Maybe they find opportunities in cities for work which are not available elsewhere," replied John. "We should be thinking about digging wells and planting crops in rural communities. It is how communities thrive. People would want to stay in their villages rather than migrate to the cities causing congestion on the streets and housing shortages."

"It requires careful planning and we don't have the luxury of time," said George. "We are in war mode."

It took about twenty minutes from the time they left the hotel to arrive at the ambassador's residence. The dwelling was a large colonial mansion, imposing on its surroundings and completely out of place amongst the local architecture. l. Beggars and hawkers blocked the huge wrought iron gates. The car drove through the gates, guarded by an Egyptian wearing a khaki uniform and a fez cap. The car stopped at the entrance of the mansion. George opened the door and John stepped out. He walked up a few steps into a large foyer. Inside the party was in full swing. Champagne, wine, scotch, and juices of all kinds together with food trays were being ferried from one end of the room to another. Chandeliers were in full glitter and large curving stairs added a pleasant ambience to the architecture. Panels of mahogany lined the walls, vases with fresh flowers lined the room and the hallway and a palm tree stood in the middle of the foyer, like a sentry. High society people with their elegant gowns and tuxedos engaged in small talk. The contrast with the street scene was night and day. It was a world unto itself. The sumptuous meal was followed by dessert of fresh pie and ice cream. Dancing followed and John was introduced to a few people, including the ambassador and his lovely and witty wife, Jillian. The evening was one of satisfying stomachs and much-added waistlines. John had never seen such gluttony in his life.

A portly man wearing a cream-colored suit with a black bow tie and smoking a Havana cigar tapped John's shoulder. John spun around.

"Sid Carter—Egyptian Date Company," he said, extending his hand.

"Reverend John Wilson, chaplain of Giza and Helwan," John introduced himself while accepting Sid's hand.

"Ah, a reverend, but not in uniform," said Sid with a hearty laugh. "That would be cause for dismissal, old chap."

"I know," said John. "Thank God I am not in the army, otherwise I would be court martialed and dismissed forthright."

Smoke from Sid's Havana made John's eyes water.

"Do you mind not blowing that smoke in my face?" John tersely asked.

"Yes, of course. I am so sorry." Sid laughed again as he stubbed his cigar using his shoe. "Did you just arrive?" inquired Sid.

"A few hours ago, from London."

"Come to think of it, I now remember you," Sid commented with a fat finger scratching his chin. "Weren't you at Giza where your parents were working on an archeological dig? You must remember me. I used to come to Giza to pick up dates from nearby farms of Siwa, a small oasis town just west of here toward the Libyan border. Excellent quality dates. A small seed with lots of glistening outer flesh."

"You are right," said John. "I remember you. Mustapha and I used to guess when your next visit to Giza would be. Now I don't know much about grading dates or the price, but I certainly knew about the poverty of the workers on those farms. How much did you pay them for picking dates?"

"I don't have any figures on me right now, but I can tell you that they are adequately compensated for the work they do," Sid retorted angrily, his face flushed. "In any case, they make much more money from cultivating dates than from selling trinkets and other useless things."

Now Reverend John Wilson knew an irate man when he saw one. He needed Sid to find employment for his parishioners at Giza. Most of John's parishioners were unemployed. The preparations for the war had left many farms unattended and workers laid off, but the economy was geared toward military wares. Sid was a regular churchgoer at Giza, the same church that John's parents went to, and now it had become his congregation. The church was established in the late 1800s and was built to serve the needs of explorers, traders, and the military personnel that occupied Egypt.

"I didn't mean to offend you by asking too many questions," John said apologetically. "Those that are employed at the farms are from Giza and I wanted to know whether their basic needs for food, water, and shelter are met, and if not, what can we do to help?"

"You can rest assured that I will work with you for such a noble goal to be accomplished," Sid confirmed as he placed a firm grip on John's shoulder. John sensed hollowness behind his words. "You may join me tomorrow for a trip to Siwa to inspect the date farms."

"Sure, I will come," the reverend agreed. "What time shall I get ready?"

"Ten o'clock is a good time to leave. Is that okay with you?"

"That's perfect. See you at ten."

"Now if you will excuse me, I must see my old friend James from the British Steamship Company," said Sid as he excused himself and left in a hurry toward a well-built man in a dark suit who looked to be in his mid-fifties. John walked over to Jillian, a slender woman wearing a long black shiny outfit with a pearl necklace and matching earrings. From the way she dressed and carried herself, John thought she must have excellent taste. Previously he had met her in London at the passport office when he obtained his visa.

"Hello, we meet again," said John as he politely accepted her hand.

"How are you, Reverend?" Jillian asked. "Such a pleasure to meet you again."

Talking to her, John found her to have a lot of empathy for the poor and suffering souls of Egypt, but she had little or no sympathy for her husband's derogatory views about the Egyptians in general. Jillian had started a society in London helping to house the street people.

"I want to start a society here in Egypt to help the street people find shelter," said John.

"I will help you since I have a lot of experience and know-how," said Jillian. "It will help you avoid my mistakes. The difficult part is to convince the people living on the streets to accept shelter and food. Very few will do so, and only when the weather outside gets terrible." She wiped a small tear. "More people should get involved in this noble task, this good work of the Lord." Then more tears rolled down her cheeks and she started to sob. A few guests turned around to see what was going on. Jillian felt embarrassed and excused herself.

"I will be back; don't go away," she called behind her. She headed straight up the stairs and into one of the rooms. When she returned, she stuffed something in John's hand.

"This is from me to the poor you serve," said Jillian. "Like the miracle of Christ, I hope this small amount may feed the many hungry mouths."

John took the money and thanked Jillian as she darted across the other end of the hall and disappeared out of sight behind a set of pillars. John counted the money. It was a thousand pounds.

That evening he met some other interesting people. Some were businessmen, one was a teacher, and another an entertainer for the troops. The reverend also met Andrew, assistant curator of the Cairo Museum of Antiquities.

"How are things at the museum?" asked John.

"We are being robbed right, left, and center," said Andrew, exasperated. "We don't have enough staff to start with, and those that we have are totally corrupt. Our director, Hisham, has asked for extra funding from the government, but it is always the same excuse—they don't have the funds because the war is on. We just have to do the best we can. I am most concerned about the loss of artifacts. We are losing precious history, which we will never be able to recover."

"I am familiar with the problem," said John. "My parents were archeologists working at Giza and they lost some valuable ancient Sumerian clay tablets. I suggest we meet and discuss ways of stopping this bleeding of national treasure. How about tomorrow evening at my hotel? I am at the Desert Inn. Why don't we meet at seven o'clock? Is that convenient for you?"

"Yes, that's fine with me," Andrew said with a smile.

"Now, you will have to excuse me," said John. He made his way to speak to a familiar face while Andrew made his way to speak to the ambassador. Small talk prevailed till well past midnight, when it was time for John to leave. George was not there, so he called a cab. The hawkers had gone home. The beggars remained. The cab arrived after fifteen minutes and, as it left the embassy gate, John opened the cab window and handed a bag of food to the beggars. He noticed that some beggars had fallen asleep and he wondered whether they ate anything at all that day.

Driving through the dark and deserted street, he arrived at his hotel in fewer than ten minutes. Half asleep, he fumbled out of the car. Omar, the reception clerk at the hotel, was still awake.

"Still awake, Omar?" asked John.

"Yes, a few guests have yet to arrive," Omar answered. "Maybe another hour before I close the reception." He had a smile on his face compared to when John first arrived.

"Tell me, does management pay you well to stay up this late?" asked John.

"They don't, but then jobs are scarce these days. I have a degree in mathematics from the university, but I could not get a job as a mathematician."

"I hope things will get better for you," John sympathized.

"I hope so too," said Omar. "Have a good night's sleep."

"Thanks, and goodnight." John raced up a few flights of stairs, almost tripping on a loose piece of carpet and hitting his face against the floor. Having reached the hallway, he walked half a dozen steps before he reached his room. Closing the door behind him, he switched the lights on. Noticing a piece of paper on the floor, he picked it up and opened it and started to read. As the light was dim in the room, he walked over to his bed and switched on the bedside lamp. The note was from London:

Call London—ask for Paul.

Reverend Paul Locke was John's superior, based at a church on King's Road, Chelsea. The call to London took a few minutes as the operator made the connection. At the other end was Reverend Paul.

"How are you doing, John?" Paul began.

"I am doing fine, though the heat here is stifling. It is difficult to get used to," replied John. "I am too tired to talk. It is past 1:30 in the morning and I have just come back from the ambassador's party. Was there anything urgent?"

"Be careful what you say. I have already had a call from the foreign office—they are keeping an eye on you," said

Paul, and with that the phone got cut off. A few crackles could be heard, then someone said, "Hello, hello."

John could not figure out who it was, but there was someone listening at the other end of the line. As John placed the phone on its cradle, he noticed that the carpet in his room was turned up. He thought someone must have entered his room while he was out. So, he got up and looked out of the window, drawing the curtain slightly. A few lights were on in the other rooms. He closed the curtain and his eyes spanned the room, catching a glimpse of his luggage. He noticed that one suitcase was partly open, yet he remembered having closed it before going to the ambassador's party. He walked over to it and opened it. Someone had rummaged through his baggage. He checked for missing items. Nothing seemed missing. However, his clothes were not as he had packed them before leaving London. Then he noticed the suitcase was cut at the top and there were some dark stains on the handle. Touching the stain with his index finger, it was still wet and it stained his finger red. After a few moments, he heard someone walking in the corridor. He switched off the lights, waited, and listened intently. Very quietly, someone opened the next-door room, entered it, and gently clicked the door shut. John pressed his ear to the wall, but not another sound came from the room. Suddenly he heard a drink being poured and gulped down rapidly. Following that the swish of running water filled John's ears.

"The damn razor," said the voice. Whoever it was sounded vaguely familiar. Then it all came together: it was the major.

The reverend began to wonder what the major was doing with the razor. Though it was plausible that the major was simply shaving, a thought came to John and he went to the bathroom to check whether it was his razor that the major was referring to. Perhaps he got the razor from John's bathroom. In the bathroom, John noticed some stains in the bath and on the carpet. There were drops of red on the floor and the bathtub was smeared with it. A clumsy attempt had been made to clean the stains. John checked whether his razor was still there. It was, but was stained. *What is the major looking for in my suitcase?* the reverend asked himself. He had nothing to hide. Then John realized that perhaps he was looking for Mustapha's address. John went back to the suitcase to check whether the address book was still there in the top pocket. Sure enough, it was missing. Why would the major want Mustapha's address when he had told him that he had not seen his friend for ten years? Maybe the major did not believe him. But then why was Mustapha of interest to him? Mustapha had gotten involved in activities not in the best interest of Britain. Perhaps the major wanted to speak to Mustapha about some matter that the major was not willing to discuss with John. All these thoughts raced through John's mind, yet no clear-cut answer showed itself. He thought that if he slept on it, perhaps by morning he would work it out.

Yet his mind still rumbled with misplaced thoughts. The phone call that had abruptly ended lingered in his mind. He tried to sleep but failed to do so. He decided to write a letter to Paul and pulled a chair up to his desk, took a few loose papers and a pen sitting on his writing desk, and started to write.

Dear Paul,

I am writing this letter to you since I fear other ears have been listening to our telephone conversations. Moreover, my room was broken into, and my diary is missing. I suspect Major Ross may be involved in this, and I am worried about the safety of my friend Mustapha. Also, the loss of artifacts from the museum and from archeological sites are valuable pieces of ancient Egyptian history that are being removed from here and ending up with antique dealers in London. Would you mind checking out a few dealers in London to see if you can discover who their suppliers are from Egypt? I will follow up at this end. Hope everything is well with you. Keep writing and avoid the telephone at all costs.

Regards,
Reverend John Wilson

John folded the letter in an envelope, sealed it, and left it on his desk for mailing the next day. Now exhausted, John's loud yawn brought a swift response from the major next door. He banged hard on the wall.

"Quiet!" he demanded. "There are people who want to sleep."

Tiptoeing to the bathroom, the reverend brushed his teeth and hastily shuffled into bed. This time he muted one last yawn, rubbed his tired eyes, and soon fell asleep.

He woke up early the next morning ready to venture into Siwa. Before Sid arrived, he dashed to the nearest post office to mail the letter to Reverend Locke. On his way back, he noticed something unusual that caught his eye.

Major Ross was having coffee at an outdoor café with Omar. They did not notice him and he did not draw their attention. John came back to the hotel and Sid was waiting for him in the lobby.

"Good morning, I hope I am not too late for you," said Sid.

"Not at all," the reverend replied.

"We have the whole day in front of us—that is, if we don't have one of those sandstorms blown here by the Khamsin winds. We should be back in time for supper," said Sid.

They got into Sid's newly polished Bentley. Luckily, working their way out of the city at that time of morning proved not overly treacherous.

"We will stop after about thirty minutes to stretch our legs and have a drink by the roadside," said Sid. "The early morning sun beats hard and the car does get overheated very quickly."

"It is not only the heat but also the sand that gets to me whenever I come back to Egypt," said the reverend. "It is like a giant sand oven." He wiped perspiration from his face and neck with a handkerchief.

"Hope you brought several more handkerchiefs," Sid jokes. "One won't be enough to wipe a sea of sweat off your face. It will soon be drenched before we even get to Siwa. I usually carry two or three on a hot day like today."

"Well, I should have thought of that before I left," said John. "Never mind, we can stop at the next village and pick some up. If that's alright with you."

"That's fine," Sid agreed. "We can stop and see for ourselves the life of the Egyptian peasants." He sped off down the desert road, kicking up sand in its wake. After about twenty minutes they stopped at the first village. A few rundown mud houses scattered across the landscape, together with about half a dozen frail looking donkeys lazily scavenging for grass. Small children ran around with little or no clothes on.

"What a sorry state these people are living in," John commented as he and Sid stepped out of the car and headed toward a small shop selling soda, dates, a few snacks, and some clothing.

"That's a common sight here in Egypt," Sid explained. "You will need to travel in the Nile delta to see prosperous Egyptians with large farms and decent houses. Here in the western desert, life is mere day-to-day existence."

They found an old man sitting under a tree selling Macaw parrots and religious icons. John approached him for a chat.

"How much are these parrots?" asked John.

"Each is priced differently," said the vendor.

"Why are they priced differently?" asked the reverend.

"Because each is unique," replied the vendor. "For example, if you wanted a parrot that answered the door for you with "who is there?" it is priced at 200 dinars, while the one that speaks about the world coming to an end soon is priced at 300 dinars and so on."

"What about that one at the end—the one with the red plumage?"

"That one is special—you will hear him say, 'Jesus loves you' and you will never feel depressed thinking that no one loves you in this world."

"How did it learn to say that?" asked John.

"One day when I was near a church, I went inside leaving the parrots outside," the vendor began. "But then I thought to myself, what if someone was to steal my precious possessions? What would I do without them? So, I took them inside with me. The priest did not mind as long as they were quiet. Soon one of them picked up what the priest was saying and began repeating it all the time: 'Jesus loves you.'"

How interesting, thought John.

As he walked around, from one macaw to another, John noticed that one of them had a bright yellow band around his neck. Then it said, "Where are you coming from?"

"From England," John replied. The next one he approached also spoke.

"Mind your own business," while a third one interjected with "war at El-Alamein soon." The reverend bought the one that spoke "Jesus loves you." He carried it with him in the backseat of the car, and all the way to Siwa there was a continuous chorus of "Jesus loves you." But the endearing message soon lost its flavor when John and Sid finally ordered the macaw to shut up. It quickly picked up the words "shut up" and for the rest of the trip it alternated between "Jesus loves you" and "shut up."

"Our lives on this earth are like this caged parrot," said John "We are trapped in material and carnal desires, unable to escape from it."

"I would disagree," Sid objected. "I think the parrot is quite content being in that cage. Have you ever seen a depressed parrot? I haven't seen one. I think they desire human company. If you were to let them out, they would not fly away. They are accustomed to being in the cage and would gladly go back in again."

"That is precisely my point," said John. "We have got used to life on this earth. There is no incentive to escape to the land of immortality, because we are not sure if it even exists. But I can tell you that it does exist, and although I have not seen it myself, I have at times been overcome with a feeling of certainty."

"We will never agree on this, so why don't we talk about something else? Look at this world in which we live and see if all the things around us make any sense as to the presence of a higher power," Sid argued decisively.

"The poverty, the wars, the famine, the greed, the lust—it seems the world is in a free fall, but the strong take advantage of it and make off with as much as they can carry," John concluded, wiping his forehead with his hands. "Helping yourself to more than your fair share of wealth is called greed. And you are punished by your own willfulness through pain and sorrow. It is like the devil casting a shadow on one's heart."

"As Darwin put it, it is the survival of the fittest," said Sid. "But I would further say it is the survival of the greediest."

Sid stopped the car at a village. They both got out. After wandering around the town, they enjoyed a cold drink and took a couple for the road. Arriving at Siwa, an oasis town on the edge of a sea of sand, they were surrounded by sandstone cliffs and a chalk-lined plateau abundant with palm groves. To the west of the town lay a large saltwater lake. The Romans were here, and so were the Greeks. Alexander the Great, who traveled in the fourth century

B.C., came here to consult the oracle of Amun. The geographer, Herodotus, came here during the fifth century B.C. recording the story of the invasion by King Cambyses of Persia, who set out with a 50,000-man army from Luxor to destroy the oracle at Siwa. The king and his army never made it; they were lost in the desert. In the centuries gone by, it was known as the oasis of Amun, after the sun god worshiped by the Berber tribes of the Libyan and Egyptian desert. To this day, Siwa has always been well renowned for its dates and olives. For it is here that Sid had invested a considerable fortune in date and olive farming.

"And how long have you owned farms here in Siwa?" John asked as they passed several date vendors.

"Six years," Sid answered. He continued, "The first few years were lean and hungry. It's the war that gave a jolt to my business. Although many farms have closed down because of labor shortage, I am lucky that my workers have stayed." They continued to tour the farm, Sid pointing out the differences between good quality dates and poor ones. John Wilson listened and asked questions. It took two hours to tour the one-hundred-acre farm. Then it was time to head back to Cairo. On the way back, they had a flat tire and spent half an hour repairing it with the help of several locals who had gathered around. Soon it was back to Cairo and the Desert Inn.

"Welcome back," Omar greeted them at the door.

"Any mail or phone message for me?" asked John.

"Not today, but a man wanted to see you," said Omar. "His name was Andrew. He said he met you at the party at the ambassador's house."

The reverend had forgotten about the meeting with Andrew arranged for that evening.

"Did he say where I could get in touch with him?" asked John.

"No, but he said he will be back again later this evening," said Omar.

"I will have a quick supper and be back in one hour," John said as he made a dash down the road to a local café for a quick supper of Kebab and Naan.

Later that evening he met Andrew. In order not to let Omar hear the conversation, they talked in John's room. The discussion was about the missing artifacts from the Cairo Museum and also from excavation sites all over Egypt. Andrew said it would be difficult to track down the responsible parties since people in high places—in government—were involved. In fact, he suspected some military officers were in on it too. The local Egyptians had a hand in it too, from one of the assistants of the museum, a man by the name Gamel, to the head of the ministry of antiquities, a man by the name of Elwafi.

"I suspect Sid Carter, since he used to come to Giza and is familiar with excavation work," said John.

"What about Major Ross?" asked Andrew.

"Maybe, but I think he is more interested in tracking down Mustapha, my friend," said John.

"I did not know you had a friend here."

"Don't forget I was born here," John answered.

They decided to work together to solve this loss of treasure from Egypt, but their work was to remain secret. Andrew left at about ten o'clock that evening, and John saw him off at the front steps.

“Be careful,” John warned as the sound of Andrew’s footsteps echoed down the empty street.

“I will, don’t you worry,” Andrew called back as he disappeared around the corner. As he turned a corner, he saw a man in a smart white suit with a newspaper in his hand following him.

John went back into the hotel lobby. There Omar stood at attention near the front desk.

“So, who is Andrew?” asked Omar.

“A friend from England,” John answered skeptically. “Why does it matter to you?”

“None of my business,” Omar quickly corrected himself. “Just making sure everything is alright with our guests. There are spies and undesirables in this place.”

“You don’t have to worry about me,” said John. He said goodnight and went straight to his room. Opening the door to his room and closing it behind him, John proceeded to close the shutters. The adjacent room was quiet. He checked the bathroom. Everything seemed normal. After considering the earlier suspicious activity in his room, he decided against reporting to Omar the stain on his suitcase, the missing diary, and the mess in the bathroom, in case Omar, too, was involved with the major. But John was curious as to the name of the guest next-door to him; although he was certain it was Major Ross, he wanted to be absolutely sure. The only way to find out, without Omar’s help, would be to do it himself. So, he crept down to the lobby. It was empty. This provided a good opportune moment to find out the name of the person next door. John hesitated at first, wondering if his fate was to get caught. But he plucked enough courage. Looking around he noticed there was nobody. He hesitated in case he was walking into a trap. He then snuck behind the front desk and peeked at the register. After flipping several pages until he came to the right room number, he paused.

"Ah, there—room 120, third line down. Mr. Ross," he said aloud to himself. "So, it was him. I must confront him next time I see him." Creeping silently back to his room, he noticed there was no light coming from the gap under room 120. John opened the door to his room, closed it till he heard that familiar click, and immediately locked it. His muscles ached from the day's adventures. He had picked up a grain mixture for the bird earlier and covered the cage with a dark sheet to keep the parrot quiet. He then walked across to his bed, sat down, took his shoes off. He went to the bathroom, changed into his night clothes, thumped into bed, and disappeared under the fresh, starchy sheets. After a few minutes, he popped his head from under the sheets and started to think of Ross and his motives for making off with his address book. He could not fall asleep straight away. In hindsight he thought that if only he had bolted his room, the major would have found it difficult to break in. He writhed for about an hour before finally falling asleep.

2
Meeting Mother

"Wake up," said a voice. "It is time for you to go."

"Who are you and where am I going?" asked John irritably.

"I am your friend and I am taking you to see your mother," said the placid voice.

"My mother has been dead for four years," John retorted.

"I know that," the voice answered.

"I am taking you to meet your mother in a place called the Garden of Bliss," said the voice. "It is a place like no other and a journey you will remember for the rest of your life."

"How can I be sure you are taking me to see my mother?" asked the reverend.

"Trust me," urged the voice. "I have been doing this for a long time."

"You mean I am not the first on your list," said John, rubbing his eyes.

"No, I have taken many people to the Garden of Bliss," reiterated the voice. "But you are privileged, in that your mother happens to be there. Besides, your mother wants to see you."

The voice was now soft and trusting.

John complied like a helpless victim. The vast expanse of the desert now opened in front of him. They walked many miles before reaching the outskirts of an oasis. There they stopped.

"Why have we stopped?" asked the reverend.

"Because I need to rest," said the voice.

"I am not tired," said John.

"But I am," said the voice. "After many trips to the Garden of Bliss, one would get tired. Wouldn't you agree?"

"I would think so," replied the reverend.

They rested for a few minutes and were soon on their way.

"Through the oasis and through the forest," the voice commanded.

Walking through the oasis, John noticed the palm trees were all of different colors and sizes. Some were ivory white, others crimson and black. He stopped to admire them and to touch them. Their trunks were immense, their fronds almost touching the sky, and their bark felt soft like a baby's skin.

"These palm trees are amazing," John whispered, awestruck by their magnificence.

"Yes, they receive the same water as the well you see over there." A long-silhouetted finger pointed to a well at the far corner of the oasis.

On reaching the well, John noticed the word "Zehura" etched in gold on its wall. Mustapha had talked about the well of Zehura, saying it contained the sweetest water ever to be found in any oasis. He took a peek inside and noticed it was lined with gold, twisted like a rope. Looking down the well, John saw his own reflection. *Ah, water,* he thought. He put his hand down and drew some water, which he pulled to his parched lips and swallowed.

"Yes, it does taste sweet," said John.

"It is the sweetest water," said the voice. "You will not find another well like that of Zehura."

When John looked down the well again, he noticed a clock lay immersed in it at the bottom.

"That's strange. That clock was not there when I put my hand down the well and brought up some water."

"It is after you tasted the water that the clock was put there."

The clock's ticking sound was now clear and regular.

John could not take his eyes off it. He began to wonder,

Who would put a clock at the bottom of a well? What purpose would it serve?

"Why is the clock at the bottom of the well?" John asked.

"It is to remind the wayfarers that time is precious, so don't waste it. Do something useful while still alive."

John put his hand in the well to touch the clock. The bottom of the well was not that far down. He grabbed the clock and turned it upside down. It had no bottom to it and yet nothing fell out from it. The gears and balances were large and moving. John put his finger into it. The clock stopped ticking. The reverend suddenly felt as if the whole world had stopped. Everything became confused and disorientated. Time and space became compressed. Fearing something catastrophic would happen to him, he let the clock go. It shook itself and started to tick once again, but now even faster than before. It was catching up to the time it had lost when it had stopped ticking. Time and space began to expand.

"Do good with urgency, as if this was your last day on earth," said another voice. "Do not lose a moment in slumber, futile play, or talk. The clock will soon strike noon, then there will be no escape or excuse. The wrath of the void will come with a force greater than that of a hurricane."

"Why did the clock stop and start once again?" asked John.

"The force that controls your destiny stops time," the voice answered. "In this is a message that you would understand what it would feel like if and when time would stop forever. The clock started once again because it is not for your world to end. The clock is an illusion, a projection from the 'other world' into well water, where it is reflected. What you saw was a reflection."

As John walked further, a lighted path led him to a forest. He followed it. Something caught his foot in the undergrowth. He didn't stop to look, but carried on. After a little while, a thought came to him. Perhaps he should go back and look at what caught his foot. He stopped, turned around, and walked briskly back to the spot. There lay a large, shiny, but partly rusty black metal object camouflaged by foliage. He brushed aside the foliage, picked it up, and examined it. It was a key. Now why would someone drop a large key in the middle of a forest? The question perplexed him as he began to walk a little further.

Several possible answers came to him and swirled around in his mind. Perhaps it belonged to someone who lived in the forest, but does not live there anymore. He looked around. There was no soul in sight. Or, it could have been dropped by someone accidentally and perhaps that person would return to claim it. Or lastly, he wondered if it was left for him.

He asked the guiding voice, "What is this key for?"

"For now, just accept the fact that it was left for you," said the voice. "So, take it and it will become useful later on."

John pocketed the key and carried on his journey. Then intense darkness began to grow around him. Before he knew it, a sheet of black night enveloped and engulfed him. He panicked.

"Help," he cried, "anybody there, please save me. I am lost."

"You are not lost. Don't panic; everything will be alright," the voice calmly replied. "It is a passing black mist." Dumbfounded, John had never heard of a passing black mist before. Then after a few minutes there was a small break in the mist and John looked up and saw the moon playing peek-a-boo with the clouds. Looking at his hands, he could not see them in front of him. Groping his way around, he banged his head against a tree trunk. Putting his hand to his head, he felt a painful bump. Tears cascaded down his cheeks like a waterfall. Confused and disorientated, he shouted one more time for help.

"Help me," John pleaded, his voice lost in the wilderness of space.

It went unanswered. He panicked that no one would answer his call for help this time. His own voice echoed back to him. What could he do now? He was helpless. Why had the voice abandoned him? Maybe it was responding to other issues more urgent than his walk through the forest. John decided it would be best if he stayed put till daybreak. Perhaps things will look better by morning. After a few hours having sat in one place, a clearing occurred in front of him. Walking briskly toward it, he noticed a wooden shack on his right side and a long bridge with a walled area straight ahead of him. The walled area had a large wrought iron gate. The shack had a door but no windows. He approached it with caution on all fours. As he came closer to the shack, its door opened by itself and John was drawn inside. Instantly his eyes adjusted to dimness. He looked around and noticed that in one corner were a table and a chair. No other furniture occupied the room. Through the corner of his eye, he caught something moving. It moved in the path of the light coming through the open door. Light fell on the object but failed to illuminate it. He tried hard to focus. A pretty face emerged from the light, glowing with radiance. Its eyes sparkled. Then a warm embrace enveloped him. John felt secure within its warm cocoon. After a while, the face became familiar to him.

"It is me, your mother," said the tender voice.

"I thought it was you," replied John, his heart racing with excitement. "Hello, Mother. How are you and what are you doing here?"

"I am the keeper of the garden and I live in this wooden shack," she said.

"What garden?" he enquired.

“You mean you never saw a walled area with a large iron gate?” she asked.

“Yes, I did, but I never realized that there was a garden behind the wall,” said John with a look of surprise.

“Yes, there is, but it is no ordinary garden. It is where bliss resides. It is a privileged place where only a few are admitted.”

“What is so special about this garden that only a few are admitted?” asked John, now distracted by the scent emanating from the garden.

“The colors and the scent are unbelievable,” she whispered with closed eyes, absorbing the aroma. “The Garden of Bliss and the long bridge are well documented in the Holy Scriptures. People must wait a long time for their turn before they are allowed to enter the garden. It was here that Adam made the fatal mistake of eating the forbidden fruit and fell from heaven.” Sadness wrapped around her face as she reflected on the thought. “On the outer wall stands a large mirror. This mirror does not reflect your outer body, but the status of your inner body, your soul. The thirty birds in Attar’s Conference of the birds came here in search of the *Simorgh*, the Kingbird. When they stood in front of that mirror, they discovered that they were the *Simorgh* themselves, and that they had undertaken a journey through the seven valleys, only to discover just that. So, while you are here, you, too, can stand in front of the mirror and canvass the status of your soul.”

“When I was young, you used to play practical jokes on me,” said John. “I hope it is not one of your practical jokes.”

“No, it is not,” she assured him. She took his hand and guided him over the bridge toward the mirror. Below the bridge flowed the river of immortality. A guard stood on the bridge.

"Who is he?" asked John.

"He is *Khidr.* He guards the bridge that leads to the garden."

"Why does the bridge need a guard?"

"To prevent those, want to enter the garden without permission," his mother rejoined. "The ark you see there is Noah's Ark. It comes here every day, sometimes it comes here two or three times a day bringing fresh souls, those waiting around their graves, which are specially marked with a circle of light. Only they are allowed to board the Ark. It is Noah who decides who enters and who does not enter the Ark. Once the Ark is full, it departs for the Garden of Bliss. Some souls are dropped off at the Garden of Bliss, while others go on to other stations. Souls not picked up by Ark are drowned in a sea of darkness and ignorance. Some people have gone to great lengths to search for the Ark, yet most people are unaware of what the Ark stands for—its true meaning." John's mother now made her way toward the bridge. John started to talk to Khidr. Then his mother turned.

"You wait here," she instructed as she darted across the bridge toward the wrought iron gate. John tried to follow her.

"You will need this." He half swallowed his words as he ran after her with the key. It was too late. She had crossed the bridge, the gate flew open, and she disappeared into the garden.

John came back to talk to *Khidr.* After a few minutes, his mother's sweet voice beckoned him.

"Come here, John," she said affectionately as her voice carried across the bridge without losing clarity. With his heart pounding in his chest, John ran across the bridge like a gazelle. On reaching the end of the bridge, he looked around. Noah's Ark was nowhere to be found. His eyes followed the river of immortality till it disappeared over the horizon. And there it was, THE ARK, sailing down the river and disappearing over the horizon. He waited until he could see the Ark no more. Then he turned and walked toward the iron gate. In front of him and perched on the garden wall was a mirror that his mother had talked about. He approached it. It came down from the wall. Another voice told him that it was no ordinary mirror.

"I know that, for my mother already told me," said John. He stood in front of it. After a few seconds, the mirror spoke.

"You have only accomplished half of what you had promised before you were born," said the mirror.

"I don't remember making any promises," protested John.

"You have forgotten," said the voice. "It is the world in which you are born that makes you forget your promises."

The reverend felt a well of urgency arising from within him. He wanted to run across the bridge and back to earth to try to finish what he had promised, if only he could remember what it was. Just then he remembered his mother was waiting for him at the gate and he dashed toward her.

"I have been waiting for you," she proclaimed. "Why did it take so long?"

"I checked myself in the mirror," said John. "The mirror said I have only accomplished half of what I promised."

“Do not worry about it. There is plenty of time left for accomplishments.”

“How do you know?”

“I know the secret of most things,” she whispered in a flutter of words. Her face glowed with radiance. “Mustapha lets me into his world of secrets.”

She got hold of his hand and led him into the garden. The gates shut behind them. John looked around, and it was a sight to behold.

“It’s marvelous.” Words could not begin to describe the vision as he ran from flower to flower, smelling them and picking them as he was filled with joy and laughter. “I am in paradise. What a lovely feeling.”

The birds came out and joined in. John noticed a flute appear out of nowhere. Though no one was playing it, notes effortlessly flowed from it. He noticed that flowers swayed from side to side in tune with the sound coming from the flute.

Flowers of every kind and color beyond imagination dotted the landscape. Roses, carnations, lavenders, petunias, begonias, hibiscus, and many others that he had never seen in his life were on display. He noticed that the garden had diffused light, but it didn’t form any shadows. The whole garden looked suspended in midair. Then there was the fragrance of every kind—it was a once in a lifetime treat for his senses. An orchestra of sweet smell and colors played upon his nose and eyes till John became intoxicated by it. A serene calmness descended on him as he walked around the garden. Then he saw someone familiar holding a watering can.

"Who is that person and what was he doing here?" asked John.

"He is Mustapha and he is adding scent to the flowers," his mother explained.

"Is he the same Mustapha I knew when I was little?"

"Yes, he is the same Mustapha, your childhood friend. He brought me here in the first place." The reverend almost passed out from hearing that. He took a few minutes to recover from what his mother had just told him. Then he saw Mustapha disappear behind a tree whose bark was all twisted with a thousand cuts on it. Then he remembered. It was the tree that Adam was forbidden from tasting its fruit. John wondered how Mustapha could even get close to it, and yet Adam was forbidden to venture near it. It was an act of defiance by Adam that brought him crashing down to earth. He went around the tree, but Mustapha was nowhere to be found. He shouted his name and two starlings appeared and sat on his left shoulder. John did not move. They broke into a melodious tune. John listened intently. Then they flew away, but the song they sang continued repeating itself. He hurried toward his mother, who was walking briskly for her age, and he soon caught up with her.

"That's bizarre," John considered. "One moment I see Mustapha and the next minute he does a disappearing act on me."

"Mustapha does not like talking to visitors. When he casts his glance at you, you can be assured he knows your mission and you will come to know your mission in a short time. In the meantime, have patience and do not resist anything you find unusual happening to you. It is all part of a master plan."

“And what about all this adding scent to flowers?” asked John perplexedly. “Don’t flowers already come installed with scent?”

“In the world where we came from, we do assume a lot of things. It is in this world where the color and scent are added to flowers. Flowers produce seeds. These seeds are sent to the other worlds by meteors and comets. It is only the *Rabb,* or the divine King, who makes that decision,” she elaborated with complete authority.

“Oh, that’s how it is,” John remarked. The garden once again had turned into a vast canopy of colors and scent. “How are colors and scents manufactured?”

A rose then appeared out of nowhere and landed in his hand. It was without any color. Slowly it started to fill with color. A hand appeared and it added something to the rose from a bottle. John’s nose picked up a scent. How wonderful! A rose manufactured right in front of his eyes. A voice then said:

“What’s the value of one rose? I will give you the whole garden.”

John recognized the voice instantly. It was Rumi’s voice.

“I was like you at one time, afraid of the gardener, as I picked one rose at a time. Then I asked, ‘Why can’t I have the privilege of roaming in his garden?’ A voice then told me I could. It said: ‘You need to break loose from the earthly chains that are holding you down.’ And I did just that. Now I can roam this garden without any hindrance.”

John noticed the trees filling up with leaves and then color. He rubbed his eyes. Flowers popped out from the earth. He heard a dialogue going on between the flowers and the trees. He didn't understand what they were saying, so he asked his mother.

"What are the plants saying?"

"The flowers are saying that without them the garden would be bland and lifeless—where divine love could never reside. Therefore, not a paradise for lovers. While the trees are saying that without them, there would be no shade and it is intellect that gives shade to knowledge, protecting the human lot from the poverty of ignorance."

Soon thereafter the garden went dull. The colors and fragrances disappeared.

"What's going on?" John asked as the beauty faded to gray.

"There is a party of souls at the bridge arguing with *Khidr* as to why they are not being allowed to cross the bridge and enter the garden. *Khidr* told them to check themselves out in the mirror. When they went to the mirror to check themselves out, the mirror fell off the wall and broke into a thousand pieces. Their insides were all disfigured, twisted, and ugly. The party felt unhappy the longer they stayed near the broken mirror and they wanted to run away and hide. But there was nowhere to hide. They were not fit to enter the Garden of Bliss."

"Who told *Khidr* not to let them in?" John innocently wondered.

"Mustapha did," she answered matter-of-factly. "Mustapha instructs *Khidr*, who then relates it to those that may want to cross the bridge and enter the garden. I also take my instructions from Mustapha."

"What wrong did they commit?"

"They belong to a party of war and destruction and are sent from another place, from the darkness of hell, from man's own inner self," said his mother. "This mystery will be revealed to you in good time."

An invisible hand pulled John toward the garden gate. It was time for him to leave. He stopped at the gate to admire the garden one more time. The garden smiled with a tremendous bloom and he saw the same parrot he bought at the souk sitting on the garden wall.

"Jesus loves you," it said.

"I know he does," John answered back.

Then he walked out of the garden and the wrought iron gate shut behind him. He stood in front of it momentarily savoring his time spent in the garden. He did not want to leave. He then remembered that he had the key to the garden. He put his hand in his pocket to retrieve it. After pulling it out, he inserted it into the keyhole. The key did not need to be turned for the gates to open. He was once more in the garden, admiring its beauty. Now he felt satisfied. His mother saw him and came running toward him.

"Why are you back?" she asked, visibly annoyed.

"Can't I remain here?" John begged his mother. "If you ask Mustapha, he will let me stay."

"Your time has not come yet," she insisted. "Each individual has to wait his turn and that is when the destined clock strikes noon; that is the time for you too. You are not there yet." She embraced him in a warm hug of motherly affection. Tears cascaded down his cheeks like torrential rainfall. He was speechless. Words of goodbye could not leave his tongue. Reluctantly, he left the garden and was once again in a clearing facing the wooden shack. He thought, *maybe when the mystery of the Garden of Bliss is revealed to me, there will be time to see my mother once again.* He started to walk toward the forest and the sun was just beginning its day's work. John put his hands over his eyes so as not to be blinded by its strong rays. A chill hung in the air as he pulled his blanket over him and went back to sleep. A few hours later a knock on the door startled him awake.

"It is twelve o'clock," said a gruff voice. John recognized it. It was Omar, the reception clerk.

"Just a minute," John called loudly through the closed door as he jumped out of bed and threw on his nightgown. Once his body was decently covered, he answered the door.

"I thought something had happened to you when I didn't see you for breakfast," said Omar. "You were leaving today, weren't you? Checkout time is eleven o'clock."

"Thank you for waking me up. I almost lost track of time. The long flight from England, then the party, plus the trip to Siwa was all too exhausting for me. Won't be long before I clear out." He closed the door and hurried to get changed. Putting on a *galabayyas*, he packed all his belongings, grabbed his parrot cage, and rushed downstairs for breakfast. Gobbling it down in a few minutes, he rushed outside and called a cab to the curb.

"To the train station. Please hurry," John insisted.

"Yes of course," said the driver.

On reaching the station as the final boarding call was being made, John rushed past the noisy, jostling crowd and bought himself a ticket to Helwan, an army base. He ran the final few meters to the train. Out of breath and sweating in the Cairo heat, John boarded the train with a few thousand others. The window seat looked vacant as he tried to take it. After a fierce scramble with two other men, he managed to subdue it. Luckily, he was not in his priestly garb. Wiping sweat off his forehead with his hands, he adjusted his glasses and settled down for a long ride.

3
The Base

The train heaved and whistled its way out of the station. Its engine sounded a little hoarse, as if suffering from a sore piston. Smoke covered the station like an early morning mist. The engineer was hesitant to pull the throttle due to the sheer number of people and animals crossing the tracks. He stuck his head out of the window from time to time until the train passed the outskirts of the city. Soon they were on their way, the countryside swishing past them like a fast-forwarded movie. The noise in the train was deafening because the passengers were in a singing and dancing mood. The musicians on board had brought their instruments. There were the *darbuka,* a local drum, the nay, a flute, *zummar*a, the *mashura,* and the arghul. One of them had also brought a *tabla* drum, beaten to the rhythm of the train passing over the sleeper joints. Everyone joined in a chorus and soon it became a party carriage. People from other carriages joined in the festivities, not knowing of course why, but a party is a party after all!

Some passengers hung their heads out of the windows to breathe in fresh air. A few kilometers out of the station, the engineer applied the brakes and suddenly everyone was thrust forward, then back, in one long slow motion. The lights went out. Passengers piled on top of each other. Upon realizing that there was something wrong, a few passengers tried to escape through open doors and half-broken windows. Some screamed with pain, while others moaned in frustration. Many were silent. Those that were hurt were hurt only slightly and they took the whole thing in good fun. The parrot consoled the injured with "Jesus loves you." The reverend was not hurt as he was thrust forward and ended up on the lap of a fat lady in the seat in front of him. He straightened himself, brushing the dirt of his clothes.

"I am sorry. Did you get hurt?" he asked the fat lady with a shaky voice.

"No, I did not. I have a built-in cushion—can't you see?" she retorted, pointing to the layers around her waist.

"What is going on?" John inquired.

"Something is blocking the tracks and the engineer applied the emergency brakes. Most likely the tracks are covered with sand from a sandstorm," the plump lady reasoned while straightening her blouse.

As John settled down in his seat, he felt peckish and thirsty. He glanced at his watch. It was half past twelve. He looked around the cabin for a food vendor; there was none. Poking his head out of the window, only part of the train could be seen. A ticket collector walked past.

"What is going on here? Why have we stopped?" John wanted to know.

"A sandstorm has blocked the tracks," said the ticket collector. John dismounted from the train to take a look for himself. As he walked to the front of the train, there in front of him and extending to about two or three kilometers he saw the tracks were buried in sand. The train driver got off and he threw his hands in the air as if in complete despair.

"Can't do nothing," he said. "We just have to wait till we can clear the tracks."

John noticed he had a Yorkshire accent.

"We better get the shovels out," he commanded. A group of porters and mechanics got to work immediately.

"How long will it be before we move?" asked John.

"Four to five hours," the train driver said and went back to shoveling. In the meantime, a few tribesmen with their camels were gathering around the train. John asked one of them whether there was a village nearby he could go to and look around and buy some food. They said the nearest village was about half an hour by a camel ride, but the people were not friendly.

"They are strange," said one of them.

"Mad," interjected another.

"I want to see for myself," John insisted. "Will you take me there?"

One of the tribesmen gave him a camel.

"Here, take this," he offered.

John hadn't ridden a camel since his childhood days. His earliest recollection was when he was five years old. He put the legs over the camel's back and managed to climb on. Another one of the tribesmen helped him to adjust the camel's halter. The camel gave John an arrogant look and threw him off. The tribesmen laughed their heads off.

"Ouch! That hurt," John Wilson exclaimed, rubbing his knees and elbows as he pushed himself up to his feet. His galabayyas were covered in sand.

“Here, give him this,” one of the tribesmen said, holding a bag of fodder. Reverend John Wilson held the bag under the camel’s mouth. It gingerly munched on the fodder. Having waited for a few minutes, John decided to try his luck once more. And bingo—it worked. He gave a slight tug to the halter and the beast took off with great speed. John’s arms and legs were all over the place, his heart pounded as if being hammered by a twenty-pound weight, perspiration dripped down his forehead and cheeks, and he held on for dear life. Pulling hard on the halter and nearly pulling the nose off of the beast’s face, it yelped in agony. A tribesman came to his rescue by pulling up beside John and tugging on the beast’s halter. The other tribesman had now caught up with John, laughing and singing and having a whale of a time. John felt like such a fool.

“Well done,” one tribesman sarcastically chided.

“Well done? I nearly got killed,” replied John, his hands shaking with fright.

“The camel is a temperamental creature, but a submissive one if you know how to handle it,” said the tribesman. “Gentleness is supreme when handling a camel.” He turned around to lead the rest of the tribesmen into the distant hills. John presumed he was their leader and joined up with him.

“How long have you been in this area?” asked John.

“We pass here every few days when we have a sandstorm. The train always gets stuck here, in the same spot every time. We come here to assist the passengers by taking them to the nearby villages for food and water. In that way we make a little bit of *bakhshish* for ourselves.”

John thought he seemed a decent person, although his baked face and heavily furrowed skin, together with a hooked nose, terrified him at first.

Leaving the lush Nile Valley, they entered the valley of sand and dunes. The sand was soft and deep, and the camels had difficulty navigating through the steep side of the valleys and escarpment. As they moved inland, the valleys got shallower and the sides less steep. The sun beat hard on John's parched body, slowly bleeding any ounce of energy still left in it. Perspiration was few and far between. Its cooling effect was minimal, if any. The village, once a distant mirage, was rapidly closing on them from the east. The few raggedy houses built of mud brick and straws were now distinctly visible. John's eyes were red and tired from the desert glare and the constant blowing of sand. Sweat remnants trickled down his forehead and onto his face, making him uncomfortable. The party had now reached the village. A few people came out to greet them. One of them perpetually stuck his tongue out. The other was only wearing one shoe while another had his *galabayyas* tied up to his knees. Reverend John Wilson thought it was a welcoming party of clowns. But he soon realized that the people here were somewhat crazy. Walking further down the village, the reverend noticed that the shops had nothing to sell. He dismounted his camel to enquire why there was nothing to buy.

"What do you want to buy?" one of them asked.

"A drink," John answered raspingly.

"Well, why would anybody want to buy a drink when there is a river right across the road?" the man answered the request.

That made sense to John, so he went down to the river. There was a man guarding it.

"Can I have a drink from the river?" he asked.

"No, you can't," the guard said flatly.

"Why not?"

"Because you will finish the water in this river," replied the guard. "If you want to have a drink then first you must bring water from that river. Then you must pour that water in this river. After that you can drink from it."

"Why would I not drink from that river in the first place?" John Wilson asked.

"Because you will finish the water in that river and then nobody will come to this river for a drink," answered the man. "I would then lose my job and then everybody will do as they please. The river will run out of water, people will be thirsty and all would leave the village. Then there would be no village of fools left."

So, John went to the other river, got a bucketful of water, and took it to the river. He emptied the bucket of water into the river.

"Now can I have a drink?" asked John.

"Only half of what you brought," replied the man. "Half is an endowment for future generations."

Reverend John Wilson drank some water and went down to see the rest of the town. As he passed the main square, he noticed a gathering of dogs. He asked someone what was going on.

"Some dogs that want to travel to the west are being entertained as a sort of farewell party," said one man. "They want to join their fellow dogs there. Here there is only poverty for us and the dogs. Everyone is talking about the prosperous west, where the dogs are fed, manicured, and taken on holidays. Stories coming back talk about how life's a beach out there. Most dogs want to go there."

John Wilson left as hurriedly as he got there.

On his way out of the village, he saw a dwarf with a tether around his neck being led by a donkey.

"Why are you led by a donkey?" John inquired.

"Because he is smarter than me," said the man with a grin. "If I was to tell him to take me to a particular village, he knows where it is, and he takes me there and back. If I were to tell him to take me to see my brother, he would take me there. So, you see, the donkey is smarter than me. In your country aren't you led by those smarter than yourselves?"

"No, we are not," said John thoughtfully. "We are led by ignorant donkeys. In fact, we put them there ourselves; that's the worst part of it all."

As John was leaving town, he noticed a few goats tethered to a tree. They had a funny look on their faces—a mixture of sadness and joy.

"Why are they sad and happy at the same time?" asked John Wilson of the head tribesman.

"They are in this state because half their brain is thinking about their dilemma, being tethered around a tree, nowhere to go but round and round, an utterly sad situation. The other half of their brain is thinking that if they could just free themselves from being tied, what a feeling of joy they would possess. So we have both happiness and sadness at the same time, which is quite unique."

John now understood why the tribesman had called the villagers mad.

A few miles out of the town, they watered and fed their camels in an old abandoned well halfway between the village of fools and the railway tracks. The well was about fifteen feet deep with some hand and foot holds to descend to its bottom. The tribesman filled their leather pouches with water. Each of these pouches held about two gallons of water. John took his share of well water and ate some date cakes that were offered to him. Having eaten, they were on our way out of the oasis into the harshness of the desert once again. The head of the tribesman, whom John had nicknamed Haraka, "the hurried one," said upon passing that the key that the reverend found in the forest was the one that he had dropped, and that he knew that the reverend would be walking the path and finding it. John was amazed at what he had just heard. He asked whether Haraka was in the garden that he visited and found to be so peaceful. Haraka said he had a glimpse of the garden but had not visited it. John then realized that he must be very fortunate to have visited the garden and stayed there long enough to admire it.

"Are you aware of who Mustapha is?" asked John.

"Yes, I am familiar with him. Are you looking for him?" Haraka queried.

"Yes, I am," said John.

"You will soon find him," Haraka assured him. "He is in Cairo with a group of whirling dervishes."

"But I found him in the Garden of Bliss," John said skeptically.

"He resides in many different places, including *Al-Khamosh,*" Haraka added.

"Where is that?"

“That’s a station.”

“What kind of station?” John had so many questions and learned so much that his mind could barely retain all the newfound knowledge.

“A station where there is silence, and therefore it is called El-Khamosh. It is where colors we see around us are manufactured. Some of these colors are in existence or *wujud*, while there are others that have been manufactured but not yet manifest. These are called *zuhur*. The Garden of Bliss and the station Al-Khamosh are two different places, existing one above the other, each in its own plane. Do you understand what I am saying?” asked Haraka.

“Yes… sort of,” John replied honestly. A man brought up in dogma now had to digest the science of colors. The workings of the other world was a topic he was never brought up with, nor was he allowed to speculate on. To speculate would be a great sin. John was fascinated by his talk. Like a thirsty man, John wanted to drink from Haraka’s well of knowledge.

John and the tribesman shared water, each one passing his water pouch around. They were now brethren, arriving at this world from different places, but each having been tied with a divine cord, inseparable until they rose together to another world, higher than this one.

The sky color had turned crimson and the stars looked down on the earth with glittering eyes. The tribesmen gathered their belongings and were on the way once again. The reverend wondered if the sunset and sunrise were so beautiful in this world, how were these colors mixed in other worlds in order to achieve such a beautiful outcome? He wanted to know more, but he had to be patient. For it is patience that ultimately leads to the most benefit. John wanted to have a glimpse of the workings of the other world, and then he would have fulfilled all his desires.

"What happens after you have visited *Al-Khamosh*?" asked John.

"You will visit a second station—a station of balance, *Al-Mizan*. There is a balance that exists in this world and all other worlds. This balance between right and wrong, between various numbers and letters, is what keeps the universe in perfect balance. Otherwise, it would not exist. The final stage of your journey will begin when the nightingale sings and it will be when justice flows from the station of balance to this world. All the past wrongs will be put right, until the next time when the nightingale sings again, then a similar process will occur all over again. During this time the light of the cross will merge with the light of the dervishes, and this will be the end of the present state of affairs. By that time, you would have accomplished everything you came here for in order to gain a place in the Garden of Bliss. Now the first of the two stages will begin soon."

"How soon?"

"Sooner than you think," said the guide and gave instructions to the other tribesmen, who gathered their camels, and soon the group was on its way. As they approached the tracks, he could not see the train. The tracks were clear of sand, but the train had disappeared. "You see, I told you that your journey will begin sooner than you think. The people on the train were not ready for this journey and therefore you were made to miss your train in order to undertake this journey."

“To where?” the reverend asked.

“We are going to show you, from a distance, of course, a station called Al Mizan—the second station.”

“What would happen there?” asked the reverend as he furrowed his forehead.

“Here each soul is balanced before it is put into a body at birth. The soul has a certain signature, which gives it strength and weakness. The perfect man is able to read this signature before prescribing prayers for that soul. If one practices those prayers, then the soul gets rebalanced once again. An imbalance in a soul results in all sorts of troubles and tribulations for that person in this world,” advised Haraka as he kicked some sand with his feet.

“So, it is the out of balance soul that gives man so much pain and suffering. It is then like the wheels of a car. If they are not balanced, the car steers of course and is wobbly,” the reverend clarified for himself.

“Perfectly correct. One’s addiction for the worldly goods results in an unbalanced soul,” Haraka added to the thought. “By balancing the soul, one also balances the intellect. Thus, a sound intellect distinguishes between right and wrong.” Haraka concluded.

The stars were out in their full regalia. John stared at each one of them in turn. He observed the constellations as they descended into him, until he felt their power in his bosom. They left their inscription in him for him to decipher. Then they ascended back to their original places in the cosmos. Each constellation undertook this journey to him and into him, and they left as fast as they came. It took less than a millisecond for the entire group of constellations to leave their transcriptions in him. John wanted more of it. He wished for more, but a dark patch filled the sky instantly.

"Kafir, kafir," a voice suddenly rang out from the bleak expanse. Before he knew what was happening, a knife was held at his throat.

"Let me go, let me go," Reverend John Wilson screamed in agony. The other tribesmen quickly came to his rescue.

"He is not kafir, not a kafir," one of them appealed to the knife-wielding tribesman.

"He is asking for more and more, never satisfied," the man argued.

"No—he was drunk with the experience—he just asked for a little more," said another, pleading on John's behalf. The knife-wielding man was quickly subdued and the incident was forgotten. But the experience left a mark on John's consciousness as he realized that he should be satisfied with what he got and not to ask for more. For greed is punishable by death. He asked Haraka to explain the experience since he did not understand what it meant.

"It will all become clear to you at *Al-Khamosh*," he said.

The chill of night enveloped them and John lit a campfire and warmed himself next to the glowing embers.

The camels were left with Haraka's friend at an oasis some five miles away. The night was cool and the company was in a jubilant mood, singing and dancing their way to the station. They carried flaming torches made from paraffin wax at the end of a long branch of an acacia tree. These torches provided a brilliant light, which made the trek through the desert easier in the blackness. Halfway through the journey, an overhead streak of gold drew his eyes away from the road.

"Look, there it is—the station of *Al Khamosh,*" Haraka proclaimed.

As Reverend Wilson scanned the distant horizon, he could see the outlines of the station glittering in the desert night sky. There were a few stars in the night and the moon was absent, and this made the station stand out brilliantly. Varied colors of red and yellow and green resembled a fallen star from the sky.

"It's radiant," John breathlessly whispered.

"It's the most beautiful place on earth you will ever visit," said Haraka.

Their pace quickened, as if they were being pulled toward the station. When they got there, they removed their sandals. Walking barefoot, and approaching the underbelly of the station, they felt a sense of awe and reverence, a one-time experience. Its shape and color changed a dozen times in the few minutes of staring at it. Then it came on them suddenly. A huge red, green, and yellow dome made up of pure light soon enveloped them. It was divided into three large cubicles—some eight by ten meters. The walls looked solid, yet one could walk through them. John stepped through the dome, passing from cubicle to cubicle. He touched its walls and floor. There was nothing there. Yet he did not fall through the floor. It was a hologram station. John wondered where the light was coming from. He looked above into the night sky. There, far beyond the cluster of stars called the Pegasus, a brilliant white light emerged from nowhere and was coming toward him.

“There is nothing here, yet I can see beyond this wall,” John said. The station then began to rise and leave them as quickly as it had descended on to them. They all looked in amazement as the station disappeared from sight.

Having made their way back to the train tracks, they waited for the next train. It came, but a few minutes late. Haraka flagged it and it responded with a loud, halting screech. Haraka had a word with the driver and John was allowed to board. The guard blew his whistle and the train heaved its way slowly through dunes and wadis. It picked up speed. Soon villages appeared and disappeared with lightning. They reached the base. The porters collected the reverend’s baggage and made their way to the army barracks. There the commanding officer waited to welcome the new arrivals.

“Welcome to the base,” he greeted the group. “Sometimes it does feel like hell in here. But we are a friendly bunch here and we will make your life as comfortable as possible, plus we have a fantastic cook. You will enjoy his meals.” A quick tour of the base at first sight indicated a huge and sprawling area filled with tanks, airplanes, metal workshops, and a large heap of scrap metal. It was surrounded by barbed wire. Men, tanks, and planes were caged within like animals. Outside the local Egyptians engaged in menial jobs, children begged for food, and women were masked behind veils, going about their daily routine of shopping and cleaning. At night the searchlights would keep the intruders off the base.

“This barbed wire, the tanks, the artillery pieces, the scrap metal—it is certainly not a welcoming place,” John commented with a touch of sarcasm.

"Well, you will soon get used to it," said the commanding officer.

"I will have to; I have no choice. By the way, where are my sleeping quarters and the mess hall?"

"Follow me. Your home is a two-bedroom unit, and the mess hall is attached to that unit. It holds about a hundred people." The officer took him through the lined-up tanks and artillery pieces and past the airman's billets. At the far end, close to the south entrance, stood a hall and a two-bedroom unit. It displayed a small patch of garden next to it. It was a small vegetable garden. John was delighted to find that he could put his green thumb to use in the garden.

"Jolly good," said John. "Much more than I anticipated. I suppose I will be right at home here." The commanding officer took his luggage in the unit and left.

"See you at mass on Sunday," said John.

"Of course, you will; we are a rowdy bunch," said the commanding officer as he left.

It was on one serene evening when he took his daily stroll around the base that Reverend Wilson found a young boy lying in a pool of blood outside the barbed wire fence on the south side of the base. John ran through the gates, turned left, and a few meters from the gate the boy was smothered in red plasma, hardly breathing, groaning inaudible words. The boy was still alive when John got to him, and John managed to gather a few words from him before he died.

"Latifa sends salaam, salaam…" and he closed his eyes for the last time. John carried the boy through the gates into the first aid center of the base. There the medical staff attended to him. There was nothing left to do for the boy.

John carried the child's body to his mother. Her name was Latifa. She was greatly distressed at having lost her only son. Little did anyone realize then that she would one day be instrumental in removing the colonial yoke from her people's necks. Next day an enquiry was held to determine the cause of death. A bullet wound was discovered in the chest and the sentry on duty admitted to firing that fatal shot.

"He was stealing scrap metal," the sentry argued, defending his actions. "I did not see whether it was a child or an adult. I just fired. That's my duty, to keep intruders off the base."

"Why didn't you shout for him to stop before firing?" John demanded.

"Because it was not in my manual. My manual says that I am supposed to fire at the first sight or sound of an intruder."

"Is it not callusing of you to fire your weapon when you know that children are more likely to be nearby? After all, the children are after scrap metal, a harmless activity, and no threat to the base," said John.

The commanding officer issued his verdict. Accidental death. No reprimand and no change in the policy of lethal force for intruders.

Reverend Wilson felt uncomfortable with the ruling. He made his views known to the commanding officer, but was told that the inquiry was upheld and a judgment issued. There was to be no further discussion. Matter was closed.

John attended the child's funeral with the rest of the family members. He read a short verse from the Bible:

"God remembers those who suffer; he does not forget their cry, and he punishes those who wrong them. Amen."

For the next few days, Reverend Wilson did not go out much. He shrouded himself with the walls of his room for most of the day. In fact, some soldiers came to see him and talk to him about the loss of the young boy and how traumatic it was for his parents. He ventured out to get supplies from the local food store located within the base. It was one of his days as a recluse that he noticed a piece of paper fly through an open window. The macaw went crazy, chasing the paper all over the room.

"Stop, stop!" cried the reverend at the macaw. But it continued to chase the paper. A voice interrupted him, saying, "Let the paper do its job. It is making a list of your worldly possessions."

"As you can see, I don't have much—only a few clothes, a bed, and a chest of drawers," said the reverend.

"Far too many clothes," replied the voice. The next day John decided to heed the message of the voice and gave most of his clothes away to the Egyptian workers at the base. The piece of paper never came back again.

He felt good about that. As the days passed in prayer and preaching, he realized that his relationship grew even tenser with the rest of the army. They kept on firing at innocent civilians and children and he had to intervene regularly on their behalf. But he kept a cheerful disposition and never raised his voice or argued when harassed by the men. Many even went so far as to call him a traitor. Some nights when the searchlights were not switched on, he used to venture out. Near the place where the local boy was killed, he tossed a few scrap metal pieces to the boys who were waiting there. Soon a crowd of boys had gathered and caused a commotion. Before the sentry noticed him, John took cover inside the mess hall and pretended he was reading the Bible.

"Is there anything wrong?" asked the reverend of a rushing soldier.

"Those boys are at it again. Stealing from the yard. Someone will get killed again," he spat as he ran toward the fence.

"Boys will be boys; leave them alone," John urgently called back to the soldier. He never knew whether his words got through to the rushing soldier, but he was unaware of anyone being killed that day. He presumed after the earlier incident the sentry would have learnt his lesson not to fire indiscriminately at the intruders.

The following morning at breakfast, there was talk that a single engine spitfire had gone down in the desert close to the base and that a search party was sent out to locate the airman. Three soldiers, John Wilson, and two Egyptian trackers, one by the name of Abdel Saleh—a brilliant tracker—were part of the search party. They left sometime that afternoon. After leaving the base, the search party took a westerly route. Traveling for about an hour and a half by camel, they spotted something on the horizon.

"What's that?" asked one of the tribesmen.

"It looks like a fire," exclaimed Abdel Saleh. They quickened their pace to reach the site of the fire, about four hundred meters away. When they got there, a single-seater plane was on fire. The pilot was nowhere to be found. After examining the wreckage, the party concluded that the pilot must have parachuted out of the plane before it crashed.

They searched the desert at a frantic pace to locate the pilot. He was nowhere to be found. Night was closing in fast.

"We will have to wait till the morning," Abdel Saleh concluded when weariness set in. They lit a campfire and waited till the first light of dawn. One of them, Abdel Saleh, took off by himself, while others were all still asleep, except Abdullah, who watched Abdel Saleh go. Abdullah awakened John.

"He is a good tracker," said Abdullah to John. "He will find the pilot in no time." They waited for about three hours for Abdel Saleh to return. The tracker had followed the foot tracks for several miles to a piece of large rock. The wind weathered it into a rounded appearance and it reflected sunlight like a crystal. As he came close to it, he noticed an opening in it. He entered it. It was a cave, dark and uninviting. Suddenly some flapping of wings drew his attention as his eyes slowly adjusted to the darkness. He had disturbed the bats, he realized. They began flying all over the cave. There must have been hundreds of them from the noise they created. Abdel looked around for signs of the pilot. He was nowhere to be found. He ventured further into the cave. The bats followed him. He tried to push them away, but they persisted to envelop him. He cried. Hundreds of them descended on him like a swarm of bees. They bit him all over his body until blood oozed from the flesh wounds. He writhed in pain, but his cries went unanswered. The pilot stood still in the corner of the cave, frozen with fear. Abdel pushed himself up, stumbled, and got up again. His eyes were now familiar with the darkness in the cave. Cautiously, he moved forward. The bats continued to devour him alive. He waved his arms in desperation, trying to fend them off. They relentlessly carried on their attack. He struggled and stumbled one more time. That was the last time he would get up. Someone rushed to his rescue. It was the pilot of the plane, now feeling a little braver. He had a flashlight in his hand and swung it at the bats, waving them away from him and the tracker. He switched on his flashlight. The bats flew away in fright. He left the flashlight on and attended to the wounds of the tracker.

He carried with him a small first aid kit, and he applied the antiseptic on the wounds. They were deep, open, and discharging blood. The man was in agony. He saw terror in his eyes, and he opened his mouth to speak a few words, but could not. Then he gave a deep sigh and slumped his head sideways. He was dead. The pilot dragged him by putting his hand under his arms and took him to the entrance of the cave. The pilot could now see his face. It was dark and rugged, with bite marks all over his face and his arms, still oozing. Meanwhile, the rest of the party decided to follow Abdel Saleh's footprints, since he had gone for a few hours and did not know what had happened to him. Soon they arrived at the huge crystal shaped rock. They waved, having noticed a figure against the rock.

The pilot waved back. He waited for the distant figures to appear closer. He waved again to make sure they knew he was still there. Before too long, John and his party made their way toward the cave.

John could not believe his eyes. It was George the taxi driver.

"What are you doing here and what happened to him?" asked the reverend as his finger shakily pointed to the tracker lying motionless on the ground.

"I could not save him. The bats got to him before I did. He died of his wounds. I am so sorry," said the pilot. "As for me, I decided to go for a spin in my plane and soon I was in trouble. The engine began to fail. I parachuted out when I saw some lights on the ground. I thought it would be safe to land here. At least I was certain of being rescued." John thought about this coincidence. Suspicion swirled in his head. A lot of questions went unanswered.

"What if I told you that this was all setup?" John asked George.

"There is nothing like a setup in this life. Everything you see and come across has been placed where it is supposed to be placed. All events are preplanned and destined to happen. Take comfort from that; you are amongst people you know and trust. Let every other thought disappear from your mind."

But the reverend was not about to buy this explanation for the second time around. Already he endured the incident where the train was stopped by sand on the tracks and the tribesmen were sent to take him to a village and thereby miss that train. Now George, the taxi driver, falls from the sky with a parachute, close to a base to be rescued by John and his party. Something did not make sense and he was determined to find out.

They buried the tracker at the entrance of the cave. A signpost read: "Here lies one who succumbs to the evil ones—those that couldn't see the 'light of day.'" After the burial was over, George put his arm on John's shoulder.

"John, my friend, it is not good that you know too much. Otherwise, you will be an unwilling participant rather than a willing one. Accept it. But in the larger scheme of things—which you will come to know soon—you will play a noble role. Of this, I can assure you about."

With George's words, John Wilson embraced comfort—though not entirely satisfied—but he had no choice but to accept George's explanation. They marched on till a distant light appeared on the horizon. They had arrived safely at the Helwan base. Soon George was in demand. Everyone wanted to know how he survived the crash, where he took shelter, and where he found the water to sustain him for three days in the desert. As he related his story, John Wilson became intrigued by one specific thing he said. It was when he was talking about water, he said that inside the cave where he took shelter a stream flowed, and yet he could not find where the water was coming from. It flowed for a certain length and then it disappeared underground. As he searched the cave, he came across a well. In it was a large clock, with a loud ticking noise. The dial moved slowly, almost as if standing still. All the while he was there it had moved only a minute. The side of the well was lined with gold. The water was clear and sweet. He drank as much as he could and sat near it most of the time. From time to time, he ventured to the mouth of the cave to see if anyone had come to rescue him.

"What else did you see in that cave?" John inquired eagerly.

"A lighted path led from the well, but it came to a stop abruptly at the wall. I touched the wall of the cave. There was nothing unusual about it. I did not have the courage to go and explore the rest of the cave. The ticking noise bothered me," he continued, "I tried to find a way to stop it. As soon as I put my hand in the well, the clock jumped out of the well and hung itself on the wall. I approached it and looked at it. The dial was now bright and shiny. The hour and the minute hand were both close to twelve o'clock. High noon, I thought. The second hand hardly moved. Then a voice said to me, 'The hour of judgment is at hand.' I asked what the meaning of that was. The voice replied, 'Death and destruction'."

"Did you wonder why the clock was there in the first place?" asked John.

"Yes, I wondered and I thought it must be an illusion. You know how the desert heat can sometimes play tricks with your mind. Although it was cool in the cave, I was terribly dehydrated from days of wandering in the desert after my plane hit the ground and burst into flames. But everything does begin to make sense—the war, the tracker's death by those that 'can't stand the light,' and then me falling out of the sky close to the base so that I can get rescued. Then I saw the clock disappear into the well and I noticed a glow of light on the wall. I looked around to see where the light was coming from. It was coming from a hole in the roof and it came straight down, bent a little, and hit the wall. It was pure white light. It began to dance as I approached it. Then it stopped moving. I placed my hand on the wall. It felt warm, as if the walls were radiating heat. I moved my hand. The light moved once more and disappeared into the well. I went to the well to look where it went. The bottom of the well was now luminous. I brought out my rosary and recited a small prayer and then there on the wall I saw a figure of Virgin Mary. Shaking like a leaf, I could not control myself. I had tears running down my face.

“She said to me, ‘Do not fear me. I have come to help. Everything will be alright if you do as I tell you.’ Then she held out her hand. Out of it flowed a ray of light. It entered the well and disappeared down into its abyss. So, I looked down the well. There I saw the clock once again. The hour and minute hand were still close to twelve o’clock. I asked Virgin Mary what it meant. She said the noon hour is the hour of redemption, of war, of hell. She told me not to take part in the war. She said it was not for me but for sinners. She then disappeared. The cave was plunged into darkness. I went to the cave entrance. There I noticed someone approaching the cave. I was too scared, so I ran toward the back of the cave. I heard some noise of flapping wings. I looked up and saw some bats hanging upside down. I switched on my flashlight. The light reflected off their eyes. Their eyes were bloodshot and they did not move. I heard cries coming from near the entrance and froze with fear that death was stalking me. I finally walked hesitantly toward the entrance. There I saw someone struggling and yelling, ‘Please help me, please help me!’

“The sound of flapping wings and cries of help terrified me. I had my flashlight. I waved it to strike the bats. They kept coming at me with screeching sounds and lethal fangs. I hit some of them. A few of them lay dead from my strikes. A few flew away terrified. I approached the man, lying in a pool of blood, and attended to his wounds. He did not survive. I dragged him out of the cave. The pain on his face was still visible. Those that were afraid of ‘the light’ had got to him before I could. I walked away from the cave. A few meters away from it, I turned around. The cave had disappeared. There was only a sea of sand as far as the eyes could see, but no cave or boulder. I wondered where I was taking shelter. I have no rational explanation, except that I was saved by being in a cave. And thank God I had my flashlight with me; otherwise, I would have been killed by the bats."

"We all have to carry an internal 'light.' It is the only thing that protects us," said John.

A few days had passed when Reverend John Wilson got a letter from London. He opened it. It was from Reverend Locke:

Dear John,

Thank you, for your letter... The weather here in London is as usual at this time of the year, wet and windy... The congregation held a christening yesterday and the mood was joyous. Forgive me for replying a little late, for I had to pursue the enquiry you suggested.... I found some interesting things and in short, I would say that the dates have been picked and the pickers are many.

Yours sincerely,
Reverend Locke

"The dates have been picked and the pickers are many." *Just as I thought. Sid must be involved in this,* the reverend mused. *But who are the other pickers besides Sid?* He could not figure it out yet. The next day a military vehicle was leaving for Cairo. He hitched a ride. He went to see Sid Carter.

Arriving in Cairo, Reverend Wilson went to the offices of the Egyptian Date Company, located near the main railway station.

"I have come to see Sid," he said when he stopped at the reception desk.

"He is not in," said the receptionist. "He left town today and he will be back tomorrow. Anything I may help you with?" she offered politely. The receptionist was an English woman in her mid-thirties.

"Yes, you may," John schemed. "I am looking to ship some dates to my friend in London, and I wonder if you would be able to arrange it for me."

"Yes, of course. But you will have to speak to Sid for that," she answered. "Why don't you come back tomorrow, and I am sure Sid would be delighted to accommodate your request."

"All right, tomorrow. I will be here at eleven o'clock. Tell Sid it was Reverend John Wilson." And he left.

The next morning John arrived at the Egyptian Date Company's offices and met Sid Carter. John told him that he wanted to send a parcel of dates to Reverend Locke. Sid obliged to send it to London on one condition: that the parcel was picked up from his agent at the East London docks. John agreed to this, then paid a few pounds for the dates and for shipping.

"One more request I have to make, Sid."

"What is it?" said Sid, irritated.

"Could you possibly employ two of my parishioners from Giza at your shipping warehouse here in Cairo? They are desperate for work, and their families are in bad shape."

"We are already overstaffed. But send them to me tomorrow and I will see what I can do for them." Sid obliged.

"Thanks much," said John and he left.

A few days later, Reverend Locke picked up the parcel of dates from the agent on the East London docks. On it there were a few markings, which he noted. There was the date, followed by the letters XXL, followed by some numbers, and then the letters AQ. He made a note of these and sent them to John at the Hellwan base.

Dear John,

I have received your parcel of dates. Thank you very much for this kind gesture. I must tell you that the customs officer at the East London docks asked me whether I minded if he opened the small wooden crate. I said not at all. He opened the crate in front of me. Inside were fresh glistening dates. I took one and offered some to the customs officer. He was glad to sample the dates. He closed the crate, and I took it to my office in the church. Opening the crate, I noticed there was a false bottom to it. I took a pair of pliers and pulled out a few nails. There, stuffed with paper, was indeed a false bottom. Make a note of the markings on the crate: 1939—XXL—632334351—AQ.

Do take care and write soon.
Regards,
Reverend Locke

He phoned a travel agent in Cairo to book a flight to London. He said it was urgent. The agent told him the flights were full and London was in the middle of German aerial bombardment and emergency only flights were allowed entrance. A few days had passed before he heard from the agent. He had managed to get him on a flight leaving in a few days. He told John he should be in Cairo by the weekend and that John should pick up his ticket at the agent's office on Salem Street. He packed his bags in a hurry and took the first train from Helwan on Saturday morning. The macaw he left with an Egyptian worker at the base. By this time the macaw had picked up a few more choice words and was a delight to the soldiers. Some taught him a few swear words, while others were thrilled to imitate him. The train arrived in Cairo at noon. He took a cab to his hotel where Omar greeted him.

"Is everything okay?" asked Omar.

"Yes," John answered simply.

"Your friend Andrew called here; he said you were coming this morning," said Omar.

"Yes, I told him that I was arriving. Did he say when he will be back?"

"He said later on this evening."

Later that evening, Andrew came for a visit. They discussed Reverend Locke's letter, what it meant, and whether the people in the Ministry of Culture were involved with Sid. That evening they went to the Ministry's offices. There they went through each and every employee's desk and pulled out drawers looking for documents linking any of them with the Egyptian Date Company. In one drawer they found a memo which read:

"In the royal palms lives the secret of the pyramids." No signature on it. Andrew knew whom the desk belonged to. She was an Egyptian who had returned to Cairo having studied in London. Her name was Halima.

"I will have her tailed," said Andrew. "We will soon find out whether she has connections with Sid." Andrew later found out the following week that Halima had connections to Omar. Now he had to prove that Omar was colluding with Sid, and that would complete the circle of suspicion. However, this would be more difficult than it seemed. Omar had been well trained in losing those that tailed him. When followed, he disappeared down alleyways and narrow side streets, through the back of cafés and through mosques. He could be seen with different people, some in the army and some in the civil service. One day, when Omar was having coffee with an army officer, Andrew paid a young boy some shillings to find out what they were talking about. The young boy observed them from a distance for a few minutes. To get closer to Omar, he approached a couple sitting behind them for some money while cleaning their shoes. He was there long enough to hear that they were talking about some truck leaving Giza at dawn the next day for Sid's Cairo warehouse. Andrew made his way by car to Giza. At Giza, the Egyptian Date Company truck loaded large crates of cargo. He followed him to Sid's warehouse in suburban Cairo, where the crates were unloaded and repacked. Waiting in his car, Andrew observed what was going on. Finally, he got out of his car and approached one of the workers.

"Where are you shipping these crates to?" he asked.

“Who are you and why do you want to know?” asked one worker.

“Just curious. I know Sid, who owns the company,” Andrew answered smartly.

“Well, they go all over the world,” said the worker. “They go to the port of Alexandria first, and from there it is shipped all over the world. Some of them go to Sid’s office before being shipped.”

This is what Andrew was looking for—a staging area for some crates where the false bottom would be opened, stuffed with the artifacts, marked with a special code, and shipped.

“And how do you keep the dates fresh in these crates?” asked Andrew.

“By not sealing it completely, we allow enough air to circulate,” replied the worker.

Andrew made his way back to the hotel to find John prepared with an update on what he had just discovered.

4
To London

Arriving in London in mid-November, with the wailing sirens, the sound of fighter planes, and a slow drizzle of rain, it was indeed a dismal homecoming. John had arrived to celebrate Christmas in London and do some investigating for himself. Reverend Locke had made a little headway in determining where the date crates with false bottoms were ending up, but could not say for sure that there were any artifacts in them.

Driving through London, he noticed rows and rows of houses flattened by German bombs. There were a few children playing in the rubble, oblivious to the danger from the German warplanes. A few horse carts could be seen, piled with people's possessions. However, most people were scavenging whatever they could salvage from their bombed-out houses. Fires engulfed the homes and water pipes burst in a sprayed frenzy. Some roads were in knee-deep water. Sirens sounded and people generally looked despondent and tired. There was a stench of rotting bodies combined with a smell from a burst gas main.

The cab dropped him at the King's Road church. Outside the church were a few police cars and yellow tape around the main gate. It read, "Police lines—do not cross."

"What's going on?" John asked one bystander.

"I think a body was recovered from the church. The police are not saying much. We have been told to stay behind the yellow tape," said the bystander.

"My goodness, what a tragedy. I arrived a little while ago from Egypt," said the reverend sympathetically.

The reverend then made his way to a policeman standing in front of the yellow tape.

"Hello, I am Reverend Wilson. Is anything the matter?" John asked.

"Do you happen to know the Reverend Locke?" asked the policeman.

"Yes, in fact I do. Is there anything wrong with him?" asked John, perplexed by the officer's question.

"I better refer you to Inspector White," said the policeman as he went inside the church to get the inspector.

"Are you Reverend Wilson?" asked Inspector White.

"Yes I am."

"Then please accompany me. I see your name on his correspondence. Do you know whether the reverend had any enemies?"

"Not as far as I know. He was well liked."

"Yes, but what about date crates and the artifact smuggling going on in Egypt?" the inspector asked point-blank. "We know from your correspondence, which we found in Reverend Locke's desk, that he knew that a smuggling ring existed within the antique dealers. You know how the smugglers get even when they suspect someone snooping around. Do you know anything about Tim Hardy, the cook?"

"No more than what Reverend Locke told me. He said Mr. Hardy was a reliable, honest person. I would not suspect him for anything suspicious."

"We want to rule him out. Just a routine."

"Rule him out for what?"

"The case is under investigation right now, so I cannot disclose information at this time." John stood there a moment confused by the questions, but tossed the thoughts out of his mind as he headed home.

Frantic effort was made to locate the cook. All last names with "Hardy" were looked up in the directory. Some had moved overseas while others were dead. Having located someone by the name of Clare Hardy, then came the breakthrough the detectives were looking for. Clare said she knew a cook by the name of Tim. He was her distant cousin. She said that Tim's sister was living in Battersea. The detectives located Tim's sister, Betty Hardy. A police car arrived at her home and they found Tim sitting down for supper. He was brought to the police station for questioning.

"What time did you leave the vicarage?" asked Henry Wise, the police officer in charge of the investigation.

"About half past seven," said Hardy.

"Did you see the Vicar before you left?"

"No, I did not. I thought he was asleep."

"Is he not normally awake before you go?" asked Henry doubtfully.

"Sometimes. At other times he sleeps in till about eight o'clock. I make his breakfast and leave," Hardy expounded.

"Did you talk to anyone that morning?" The interrogation grew intense as the questions continued.

"Not anyone in particular. There was a vagrant near the vicarage, and he wanted to know if I had any leftovers from the previous night. I gave some leftovers and then the vagrant left," Hardy innocently replied.

"What did he look like?"

"Like all vagrants do—shabbily dressed."

"Where did he go next? I mean, did he go to the back alley?"

"I don't know…he went across the road, and I turned left to go to my sister's house. This was at 7:30 a.m. The last I saw the vagrant was at that time," Hardy said with a confirmed nod.

"Has this vagrant been here before? Is he familiar to you?" the inspector persisted.

"No, this is the first I have seen him; there were other vagrants before, but this one was not the one familiar to me. I used to feed the leftovers to Izzy, the vicar's cat. Today Izzy was not around, so I gave his share to this vagrant." Another officer whispered a few words into Henry's ear and interrupted their conversation.

"Can you identify him?"

"Sure, I can; I remember him distinctly," Hardy answered.

A short while later they picked up the vagrant and brought him in for questioning.

"Is this the man you saw this morning and gave food to?" Henry asked Hardy.

"Yes, that's him," replied Hardy with conviction.

"Tell me your name," the inspector demanded of the vagrant.

"Harry," the vagrant replied meekly.

"Now tell me where you were this morning at about seven o'clock."

"I was, as I am every morning, collecting bottles."

"How well do you know Reverend Locke?"

"I don't know him. It is the first time I was near this church," Harry pleaded.

"We found Reverend Locke's body this morning. Do you know anything about it?"

"If I knew, I would tell you right now. But I don't. You see, I only collect bottles and trash, which is of no use to others. There was a man who was snooping around the church this morning. He was driving a black car—I couldn't tell the model—but he was well dressed and wore a gray suit and a black tie."

"Any unusual features like a mustache, a beard, or long hair?"

"Yes, he had a beard, sort of a graying at the edges. He wore glasses, black, and heavy rimmed. He was quick. I saw him jump over the fence into a waiting car and disappear as fast as a cat. I thought that was funny. Must have had a quick pardon from the vicar for his sins, I thought," said the vagrant with a nervous chuckle.

"That will be all for now. You can go." Henry opened the door for the vagrant to release him.

The sirens sounded once again and everyone took cover. The German bombers had appeared over London. The sirens sounded. The inspector and his assistant all rushed into the underground bomb shelter below the police station, while the crowd who gathered outside scrambled to the nearest safety of another underground bomb shelter. Flames leaped into the air as bomb after bomb fell on the Chelsea neighborhood. At one time, the church nearly got hit, missed by a few meters, as the army barracks next door got struck.

They rushed to help the wounded and the dying from the army barracks. Fire engines came, a crowd had gathered, and everyone was rushing, bringing buckets of water, attending to the wounded, and carrying the dead in their horse carriages for burial. For about half an hour there was chaos and mayhem in the streets. After that a siren sounded for the all clear.

The inspector then carried on with his work. They were looking for a bearded man with black, heavy rimmed glasses. Who were the vicar's enemies? Was it someone who attended his sermon regularly, an antique dealer, or a close relative trying to claim some insurance money? Or was it the vagrant, trying to cover his hind but cooking up almost a believable story? What was the vagrant doing at that time in the morning near the vicarage? These questions perplexed the inspector as he perused Reverend Locke's personnel documents, diary, and address book. From the address book, the inspector found that there was the vicar's cousin, John, who worked at the British Museum. Then there were the antique dealers of Chelsea, a tightly knit group, whose code of silence was legendary. Mrs. Johnston, whose name appeared in his diary, was not a relation, but a friend.

Reverend Locke kept a list of all his parishioners who frequented the church during Sunday service. For the inspector this was useful information. The vagrant was of interest, but probably did not commit the murder since he had no blood on his hands. Was he an accomplice? That was to be determined. What did he have to gain by the vicar's murder? Was he an antique dealer in the clothes of a vagrant? As these questions occupied the inspector's mind, as he made careful notes regarding the motive of the murder. The time that each person's whereabouts were tracked, witnesses were called upon to interview and a thorough search of the churchyard was made for any clues. The inspector was interested in the vicar's cousin, John. He would have the most to gain with the murder, since he was in charge of the Egyptian antiquities department at the British Museum. They went to see him at the British Museum. They asked his superiors if they could have a word with John. They agreed.

"Is he in serious trouble? He is the best we have," said the curator.

"For the moment, no, he is not," said Inspector Hardy.

"This way," said the curator. He led Inspector Hardy and his assistant through the hall and turned left into a door at the far end of the hallway. They arrived at John's office.

"Good morning," said Inspector Henry.

"Good morning," John greeted them, looking weary as he stretched upward.

"Have you been awake all night? Is that why you are tired?" inquired inspector Henry.

"No, my usual morning stretch. In fact, I was in bed early last night. Is anything wrong?" asked John.

"Yes. We hate to break the bad news to you, but Victor Locke is dead. We found his body this morning at the chapel." John was obviously distressed, and took a few minutes to compose himself. John was a regular churchgoer where Reverend Locke preached.

"Can you tell us anything? Were you in the vicinity of the church this morning?" asked inspector Hardy. "Take your time. I know this is distressing for you."

"No, I was not. I left my flat in Earl's Court this morning at eight o'clock, and I arrived straight to work," said John in a shaky voice, wiping tears from his eyes.

"And what time did you get here?"

"I would say 8:45."

"And you did not stop at King's Road before coming to work?"

"No, I did not," said John.

"Who saw you arrive at work?"

"You can verify that with the curator."

"That's all for now," said Henry. They left and John was still slumped in his chair looking dazed long after they left.

"What time did John arrive at work this morning," the inspector asked the curator after leaving John's office.

"The usual time," said the curator.

"What is that supposed to mean?" shot back Inspector Henry.

"I mean the usual time of 8:45 a.m."

"Are you sure about that?"

"I did not see him arrive at 8:45 a.m., but let's go and check the sign-in book and we will know for sure," and the curator led him to where the book was kept.

Inspector Hardy examined the sign-in book. It showed 8:45 a.m. as when John signed in for work.

"We will be in touch," Hardy said with finality in his voice. "One more thing before I leave. Was there anyone who saw John arrive at 8:45 a.m.?"

"There is the secretary and the assistant curator who arrive before John does. I can go and ask them."

"No, I will go and ask them. Show me where their offices are," said the inspector abruptly.

The curator led them to two doors that separated John's office from the assistant curator and his secretary.

"A quick question for you sir and madam," said the inspector, addressing the assistant curator and his secretary. "Did both of you see John arrive in this building at 8:45 a.m. as the records indicate?"

"I was making coffee at 8:35 a.m. and I was in the foyer at that time. I saw him come in around that time, but can't be too sure," said the secretary.

"What about you?" said the inspector, directing his question at the assistant curator.

"I was in my office at that time, so I can't be sure either. But I heard him open his office door; it must have been about that time. He is not usually late," said the assistant curator.

"Well, you can't be sure, can you?" said the inspector tersely.

"Can't be sure of the exact time, but close to it," answered the assistant curator.

"That's not good enough," said the inspector and he walked out of the door followed in hot pursuit by his assistant.

"We will have to pursue this further," said the inspector to his assistant. "Keep this line of inquiry open. We will see where it leads us to." He left in his black Morris Minor, snaking his way through the London traffic and arriving at the police station in time for lunch.

"There is a message for you," said the assistant commissioner.

"From whom?" asked Henry.

"From the hospital, Fulham General."

The message read: "Women admitted with cuts and bruises to both her hands. She has blood all over her. She says a dog attacked her."

"It is the breakthrough we have been waiting for," said Hardy as he picked up his hat and headed straight for the door. He climbed into his car and drove at full speed toward Fulham General. There in the emergency room, a short, thin woman wearing a white blouse and a blue skirt sat with her head in hands, sobbing uncontrollably.

"What's the matter, love?" he said gently.

"The dog bit me," she answered between choking sobs.

"Where was the dog?" asked Henry.

"Well, I was walking down King's Road when it attacked me for no reason."

"What time was that?" asked Henry.

"I don't remember, but I know it was a black vicious dog. Are you going to take him to the impound lot?"

"I don't know, but you will have to tell me a bit more. What were you doing on King's Road?"

"I usually go to church, and I prefer to walk."

"What is your name?"

"Mrs. Elaine Johnston," she said, looking down.

"How often do you go to church?" asked Henry.

"Maybe once or twice a week," Mrs. Elaine Johnston answered.

There was silence. Elaine started to cry.

"But I did not kill him," she said, still overcome with fitful weeping.

"Here use this," Henry offered as he lent her a handkerchief to wipe her face with.

"Thank you. I feel much better now," she said after a little while. Composing herself, she admitted to going to church that morning.

"There were a few people there; I was not the only one."

"What time did you leave church?"

"When it was over," replied Elaine reluctantly. She shifted her weight and fixed her eyes on her hands as she spoke.

"What time was that and were you the last to leave?" Henry pushed.

"It was eight and I was the last to leave."

"You have not answered my questions fully and you are not being honest with me, are you, Mrs. Johnston?" said the inspector forcefully. "Now what time did you leave the church?"

"Well, it was about 8:30, I would say. The last person I saw was the vagrant collecting bottles. He had a strange look on his face," said Mrs. Johnston.

"What kind of look?" asked Henry.

"Angry. I don't know," replied Mrs. Johnston, her voice smothered in annoyance. "He must be the one who murdered the vicar."

"And why would you say that?"

"Well, it was the look on his face; that angry look."

"Did he have any grudge against the vicar that you know of?" Henry asked.

"I don't know. I have never seen him before. He just happened to be there."

Inspector Hardy now knew that something was seriously wrong with Mrs. Johnston's story and thought the best course of action would be to ask the resident doctor to assess her mental condition. Dr. Young on duty washed Mrs. Johnston's wounds, dressed them, and took her into the office for a mental assessment.

"Now tell me honestly, Mrs. Johnston, how did you end up getting injured?" asked Dr. Young.

After what seemed like an eternity of silence, she opened up to Dr. Young, since inspector Hardy was not in the room.

"You can now tell me in confidence," Dr. Young gently urged.

"He raped me. He did, I swear he did," Mrs. Johnston appealed and broke into tears.

"Who raped you?" asked Dr. Young.

"Reverend Locke did," Mrs. Johnston answered.

"Are you saying he raped you in front of all the people in the congregation?" asked Dr. Young.

"No, when I was fifteen, and living in Yorkshire, Reverend Locke was a choir boy then. I do recollect him well," said Mrs. Johnston.

"How did you come again to be in the same church as him after so many years?" Dr. Young asked.

"I don't know, but I presume the good Lord wanted me to take revenge, so he must have sent me here. I don't know, I don't—" said Mrs. Johnston as her sobs grew heavier.

"Would you like to go home now that I have treated your wounds?"

"Yes, if you don't mind."

Dr Young picked up the telephone and asked for a cab to King's Road. At this time the inspector walked in.

"I will take over when you have finished," said Henry.

Dr. Young had a word with him, telling him it was not a good time to pursue the murder inquiry.

"I will see you in two days' time. I would like to assess you further," Dr. Young said to Mrs. Johnston.

"Yes, Doctor," she readily agreed.

"For now, Inspector Henry will look after you," he added. He led her out of the office accompanied by Inspector Henry to the waiting police officers in the corridor.

"She is a disturbed woman," Dr. Young warned Inspector Henry.

"I would like to charge her with murder for now, and I want a full report on her mental health for the courts," Inspector Henry ordered.

"That will be available to you after I have seen her and assessed her in two days' time," Dr. Young replied as he swung his stethoscope around his neck.

In the meantime, Mrs. Johnston was transported to a jail within the police station on King's Road.

She appeared agitated and was transferred to a local hospital, given some antipsychotic drugs, and transferred back to her cell until Dr. Young saw her in two days' time. During her time in jail, she refused to eat, muttered to herself, and walked around in circles in her cell.

"I killed him, I killed him," she was overheard as saying.

Meanwhile, that night Reverend John could not sleep, thinking about his friend Reverend Locke. Eventually he drifted into a fitful sleep. A dream came to him that night. It was his mother again.

"He missed the Ark," she told him.

"Who missed the Ark?" asked John.

"Reverend Locke did," she answered sadly. "His past was a heavy weight on his soul and therefore he was not allowed to board the Ark. His soul was left by the graveside, where it was overcome by the flood of darkness and it drowned." After she spoke, she was gone as fast as she had come. When he woke up the next morning, he was so tired that he felt lethargic and lifeless. He spent the whole day clearing up Reverend Locke's papers and other personal belongings.

The following day, he resumed his work of tracking down the antique dealers who were responsible for smuggling the Egyptian artifacts. He walked about King's Road visiting a few dealers, and then he traversed to Bayswater and visited a few more there. Wherever he went, he was shown a few objects, which were of no use to him. He employed the services of another vagrant to try and track down the smugglers.

"Will you do me a favor?" John sought out an aimless beggar.

"What favor can I do which will be worthy for a Reverend?" answered the vagrant.

"I want you to go to the back of the antique shops on King's Road and see if you can find rubbish in their crate that looks like this." John showed him pieces of a date crate with the markings of the Egyptian Date Company.

"Will do. How much?" the vagrant bartered.

"Oh yes. A quid," John offered.

The vagrant took a quid and disappeared through the back alley. Now all Reverend John had to do was to wait till he got back. He would then follow up his inquiries with the metropolitan police department in charge of stolen antiquities.

After a couple of days, the vagrant was back empty-handed.

"Nothing so far," he said, "but I will keep trying."

"How about twenty quid? Will that help to buy some food?" said John.

"That helps, but not enough," said the vagrant. "You see, I have my buddy with me and I need to give him some money too."

"How about forty quid?" John upped the price.

"Now you are talking," said the vagrant. He took the money with eagerness, stuffed it in his shirt pocket, and picked up his bundle of bottles and old clothing and left the vicarage through the back door. It was after a few days that he returned with a few pieces of wooden crate with the Egyptian Date Company markings on it.

"Where did you pick up these pieces from?" asked John.

"I found them behind a supermarket," said the vagrant.

"I said to you to search behind the antique dealers, not the supermarket," John replied flatly.

"That will be another twenty quid."

"Alright, here. Make sure you search the alleyways of the antique dealers, understand?" With the extra twenty pounds in his pocket, the vagrant took to the streets. John followed him until he disappeared into the alleyways.

After a day the vagrant faithfully returned. This time he had brought back something that John was interested in.

"Well, where did you find these this time," John asked.

"When I was at the London docks yesterday, there was an antique shop right across from the docks. The name I remember clearly was Joseph and sons, antique dealers. That's where I found these." He gave John the wooden crates with markings of the Egyptian Date Company. The markings varied from crate to crate; some had numbers entirely and others had both letters and numbers.

"Can you tell me where each one of these crates came from?"

"The clean ones came from the back of the antique shops while the dirty ones came from the grocery stores."

"Nice work," John praised him.

"It was not difficult at all. I walked the alleyway behind the antique shop, and there among the rest of the discarded boxes and other rubbish was the crate with the markings on them."

John noticed that it was the clean looking crates that had both letters and numbers on them, while the dirty looking crates had only numbers on them. Figuring out what the numbers and letters meant was the next task on his to do list. "That's all for now," John said as he dismissed the beggar.

Soon the vagrant was gone and John returned to his room wondering what to do next. He phoned one of his friends requesting how to proceed. His friend advised him to inform the inspector for antiquities at the metropolitan police station, and see what comes of it. The next day, he went to see the inspector and shared with him the whole story. The inspector listened, frowned a little in disbelief, but kept his opinion to himself, then said politely to the reverend that he will take control of the situation henceforth.

"Some dealers are vicious, not taking lightly to people prying into their little world of smuggling," warned the inspector.

John left the station and thought about whether he should inform his friend Andrew. Then he thought, it would be better not to say anything at this time, but would relate everything to Andrew when he got back to Cairo.

Christmas came, and London was still in the grips of the Luftwaffe bombers. Celebrations were curtailed and it suited John since he was in no mood to celebrate. There were no Christmas lights anywhere in London, as it was blackout time. He went to see his sister who lived in Yorkshire and there, leaving his anxieties back in London, he found some peace and time to reflect. Soon after Christmas he was back in London, and saw the two inspectors conducting the inquiries for the artifacts and handling Mrs. Johnston's case. After receiving an update, he left for Cairo. He found that the murder and the smuggling were not related. The smuggling was a highly sophisticated operation, involving the antique dealers, museums, and some crooked gangs in London acting as middlemen. However, the missing artifacts case wasn't closed yet. It had only just begun.

5
Al-Fayum

Soon after arriving in Cairo, John went to see Andrew and report to him about the theft of the artifacts. They met at a small café near the hotel. Andrew was late, trying to lose track of someone who was tracking him. And he succeeded.

"I lost him. Thank goodness," said Andrew, wiping beads of perspiration from his head.

"Lost whom? Explain yourself," said the reverend.

"Someone was trying to follow me. I bet it was someone from the museum. They know I am after the stolen artifacts," said Andrew, hyperventilating.

They discussed the progress in London.

"The police inspector has the file going and soon there will be a resolution to this matter," said the reverend.

"You mean to say that you went to London and could not resolve the matter?" said Andrew with bitterness in his voice.

"Well, there was a murder in London. I lost my mentor and friend Reverend Locke. Some deranged woman murdered him, saying that she had been raped while Locke was in the choir in Yorkshire."

"We will have to find out where these crates are coming from. Can you assign someone to watch the warehouse of the data company?" asked Andrew.

"Yes, I can send a few men from Fayum to scout the warehouse area and report anything suspicious going on there." John made travel arrangements for later that day and left for the small oasis town of Al-Fayum, about one hour's drive from Giza pyramids. He stopped at Giza to examine the excavation work going on since the time his parents last worked there. There he saw for the first time the changed landscape; the place had changed beyond recognition. More archeological activity continued and more on-site thieves were present, together with the Egyptian Date Company's ever-present truck, just as it was when he was a boy growing up under the shadow of the pyramids. John did not stay for too long, maybe about forty-five minutes. Soon he was on his way to Al-Fayum, where there was an early 1800s church still established.

It was a long, dusty journey with army trucks and commercial trucks kicking up dust storms. When he arrived at Al-Fayum, he was greeted by the small Christian community, which existed there for over a thousand years. There in the middle of the town was the church, a tiny six hundred square foot building made of wood, enclosed by a three-foot wall with a wrought iron gate. It was encircled by about twenty houses made of sand bricks and mortar. It had an adjoining office and a one-bedroom apartment attached to the east wall. This was a community of about eighty people.

Arriving at the church, he was met by a cat waiting for him at the front gate for several hours, according to the villagers. His name was Marju and he led the reverend to the church door. As he opened the door, Marju quickly darted between his feet, walked ahead of him, and stopped at the entrance while John knelt down before the altar in prayer. After his short prayer, he took a tour of the church and found it in a bad state of repair. That day a few people came to greet him and offer him food and he accepted their company. The conversation centered around building the community of Al-Fayum and finding employment for those who were out of work. During his conversation, he enquired about Marju, where he came from, and how the cat knew that he was going to arrive there as the feline waited at the church gate. He was told that Marju was found wandering amongst Giza pyramids, and that Raabia and her parents rescued it. Raabia was a resident of Al-Fayum and had lived there for some twenty years.

"He looked thin and frail," one of the worshippers began. "I guess Marju got separated from the rest of his family and lost his way or he knew that Raabia was in the vicinity of the pyramids, and therefore left the sanctuary of the pharaoh's tomb and wandered in the path of Raabia, waiting to be rescued. She brought him to Al-Fayum. Ever since then Marju has made the church his home and Raabia his friend. He waited at the church gate; we didn't know what he was waiting for. Now it all makes sense—he was waiting for you to arrive. That he led you to the church door is most unusual, for he hadn't done that for any of us."

"I will have to speak to Raabia to fill me in on the details," said John as he left the prayer hall and proceeded to his bedroom. John began by phoning a few people he had met at the ambassador's reception party, among them the head of the steam ship company.

"Hello, James, it is John. We met at the ambassador's party. Do you remember me?" asked John, his voice sounding distant due to a crackling phone line.

"Yes, of course, but you have to speak up. The line seems to be bad down here," James yelled into his end of the receiver.

"My people need jobs. Do you think you can help?" asked John.

"Of course. We need people all the time. There are always people leaving, or taking unpaid leave, so send them to me."

"Is it alright if I were to send six people?"

"Of course, it is okay. Though I need to screen them first to make sure they are suitable for the jobs. I can't promise everyone will get a job, but at least most will. Bye for now," said James as he hung up the phone. John felt over the moon. His first day at Al-Fayum, and he managed to find work for his people. The next day he asked the eldest member of the congregation to find six suitable candidates whose families had little income, and who would benefit from a job.

Next Reverend John turned his attention to the mysterious cat, and the girl called Raabia. He decided to take a walk in the village and go and visit Raabia and her family. It was Marju who led him to Arabia's house. How clever, John thought of Marju. Having arrived at her house, being greeted at the door by her father, John entered the tiny mud brick home. There he was offered some halwa and coffee. He asked to see Raabia.

"Now tell me about Marju," asked John.

"Well, my family was traveling through Giza, when we had a flat tire. My father repaired it, and out of nowhere came this thin frail looking cat. It was waiting by the side of the road. The pyramids were a short distance away. We did not know what to do with it; therefore, we decided to bring it home with us. Ever since we brought him to Al-Fayum, he has been sitting at the church gate. I have to bring food for him every day. Sometimes, I play with him. When there is a full moon, he sits near the wall of the church, and when I stroke him, he reveals to me knowledge that I never had before," said Raabia.

"What kind of knowledge?" asked John.

"Knowledge about the inside of the pyramids, the secret chambers, the pharaoh's hidden body, and other secrets that are too scary to reveal," Raabia whispered.

"Like what?" asked John.

"Like the parting of the sea," answered Raabia.

"You mean the Red Sea during the time of Moses?"

"Yes, so many people drowned in my mind as if it only happened yesterday."

"What other secrets did he tell you?"

"It is only when you look into his eyes that he can tell you the secret of eternal life, which is what the pharaohs were in constant search of."

"And what is the secret of eternal life?" asked John.

"Love of the Divine," said Raabia.

"And how do you know all this in such a short time?" John wondered. "You are only a little girl and you have so much knowledge."

"I am Raabia, who lived in Basra many centuries ago," she began. "I had many men who wanted to marry me and I said no to all of them since I was only in love with the Divine. Marju and I have a special relationship—a relationship on a higher plane, not the human or the worldly plain. When I look into Marju's eyes, I see the same knowledge that is being transmitted to him as what I have in me. It is only that he cannot verbally communicate that to me. He communicates to me through brain waves."

"He does not look into my eyes. Whenever I try to look into his eyes, he turns his face away, and his eyes focus on the horizon toward the pyramids," the reverend told her.

"He does not trust you yet, or perhaps you are not yet ready to receive that knowledge. But in time he will. He gets his knowledge from the pyramids. The knowledge that is buried in the secret chambers, and accessible only to a few. One of them being Marju, whose ancestors lived during the time of the pharaohs and were regarded by them as gods, and therefore were worshiped. Some knowledge diffuses into him while gazing at the pyramids, while other wisdom—the higher forms of it—he acquires by visiting the pyramids. Always, he has to be in the vicinity of the pyramids or in sight of the pyramids for him to absorb that knowledge. Therefore, naturally, when he looks at the pyramids, knowledge diffuses into him, and it is this knowledge that he guards so precisely," Raabia explained.

"What do I need to do to receive that eternal knowledge?" John urged.

Raabia looked at Marju and turned toward John.

"He said it is the dogma that is holding you back. Let go of dogma and you liberate your soul from its shackles." As the last word lingered in the air she disappeared into another room.

"Come back," begged her father and he threw his hands in the air. "It's God's wish." He turned to John and asked whether he could get him some more coffee.

"No thanks," said John as he took leave to go back to church. Marju stayed behind with Raabia.

"It is the dogma that is holding me back," he muttered to himself while walking back to the church. A donkey brayed nearby, and a cockerel ran across the road. He went back to the church and bought a dictionary and read the definition of dogma: an authoritative view without adequate grounds. *Now what would that be?* he thought to himself. Everything he had been taught, he accepted without questioning. Questioning was frowned upon as the work of the devil, and therefore he never questioned. But where would he start—from the beginning or from the end? He could not figure out how to start, since the analytical tools at his disposal were primitive or worn out. He left it at that. He thought Marju would provide the answer one day, if he befriended him.

A few days later, he visited the local market. Traders from around the oasis came to Al-Fayum once a week to sell and to buy. While touring the market, with all the variegated colors of costume and merchandise, he met Raabia once again.

"What brings you here?" asked Reverend John when he saw her among the crowds.

"I thought I would meet a trader who gave up the lying and cheating in business and now follows the straight and the narrow path. He related to me one day how a certain enlightened soul from the land of Hind came to him and related a verse of poetry.

"In this world, you have come and accumulated much wealth. Of all that there is, nothing belongs to you in the end. If you accumulate wealth by cheating in business, then you will fall into a perpetual cycle of birth and rebirth and the soul salvation, which is the eventual goal of all human beings, will be denied.

"With this dream, he felt sick to his stomach and thereafter did not come to market for three weeks. I found him huddled from dawn to dusk in one corner of the church." Her voice was soft and gentle as she finished the story.

"Will you take me to meet this trader," John asked hopefully.

"Of course. In the meantime, he said he has received more poetry in his dream, but he did not reveal the nature of it to me—maybe he will reveal it to you," said Raabia.

They went to see this trader who sold clay pots. His stall was full of pottery of different shades and sizes. As they sat to talk to him, he offered them some coffee and date cake. The merchant related how he continuously received this dream and each night a different subject.

"It is the same voice that I encounter each time, and the singing is done in the language of Hind and I hardly know it. But by the end of the recitation, I am able to grasp the total meaning of what I just heard," said the merchant as he sipped hot coffee. Then the subjects of tithe, the nature of the Divine, the contemplation of the Divine, and the ethical way to live were all mentioned using an allegory. This religion, the merchant said, was an everyday act of living and not one that is brought out of a closet once a week and put away in the closet for another week.

"I can understand where you are coming from. I, myself, have undergone a similar transformation, but I still keep to the church. It is, after all, a house of worship. You can incorporate this new inspiration into the teachings of the church. It is still the same message, but conveyed in a different language and flavor that seems to connect each faith like a thread running through them. Faiths are not different from each other. They are marketed as different, but truly, they are not. If you can link various faiths together and take a little from each, you would become wholesome. The rainbow is made of different colors, yet the light that produced it in the first place was that pure light. Religions are precisely like that. There is that divine light that flows through each faith, yet gives each its distinct color and flavor. You realized this; most people don't have that broad vision to grasp that, and moreover, the church leaders perpetuate this notion that faiths are separate, thus having nothing in common with each other. They compare them to soap powders, each company claiming the superior cleaning power of their product. That's why more and more people are moving away from organized religion, because of the bigotry infested within it," said Reverend John.

Raabia and John took leave of this enlightened trader and made their way toward the church. While talking about the condition of the congregation—their inherent poverty—Raabia mentioned something interesting.

"The same trader whom we met told me that a thought came to him one day that the story in the Bible about David and Goliath was a parable. Goliath is the ego within yourself, and David, who stands for the intellect, is used to destroy the ego so that you claim the kingdom of salvation of your soul. I thought that was an interesting interpretation; simpleminded folks steeped in dogma and literal translations of holy texts will not understand this. It is the Sufi way of thinking that liberates you from the shackles of dogma," said Raabia.

"I have the same inspiration from time to time, but to relate that to the churchgoers would amount to blasphemy and I would be admonished by the church. You have to keep certain things that are esoteric in nature to oneself, until the people are ready to receive it. They are only ready when their minds are sufficiently developed and it takes many centuries—and many births and rebirths—before you are either born into a faith that does make it part of their teaching or, like us, are fortunate enough to receive it and cut short our cycles of birth and rebirth," John remarked as he left the merchant to attend to some matter in church.

The next day, after sunset, when the rays of the full moon brushed the sand in a mixture of marine blue, Marju was near the church's wall and Reverend John approached him with a bowl of milk. Marju gulped it down, turned his face toward the pyramids, and gazed at it for an hour. John looked at him in amazement and wondered how many more secrets of the pyramids were left to be revealed. The reverend was a man of patience and the following day, he decided to take Marju to the pyramids. Maybe this act of kindness toward him would pay dividends. He got in his old beaten Morris Minor and drove toward the pyramids to the spot where Raabia had indicated to have found him. He let Marju out of the car and watched him trek toward the pyramids, which were four hundred yards away. John followed at a distance. To his surprise, Marju led him to a narrow opening and disappeared into it. Marju crept down a steep passage, the descending passage, whose alignment with the dragon star signified the descent of humans into darkness and evil behavior. Every inch down the descending passage, which represented each year in the life of the kingdom, the stone pathway was lined with impregnated crystals of iron that stored information digitally of life in the kingdom. Marju, whose paws had extremely sensitive nerve endings, was able to pick up the information stored within the iron crystals. He passed between two scored lines, perpendicular to the floor and extending from the floor to the roof. This alignment was recently discovered to line up with the star Alcyone in the constellation of Taurus. Marju stopped here for a few minutes.

The sacrifice ceremony of the bull, as it happened many thousands of years ago, was now being related to Marju. The sacrifice represented the atonement for one's sins and the beginning of the cycle of divine grace. Then Marju entered a passageway representing approximately six hundred and eight years, which led to the ascending chamber. The ascending chamber, now blocked by a granite plug, reminded mankind of the difficulty of entering the spiritual world without sacrifice and hardship. Then Marju managed to find a hole in the surrounding limestone large enough to crawl through it. Finally, he managed to reach the king's chamber.

Here Marju sat and waited for the pharaoh's high priest to appear—a strange figure, clothed in a long white robe with a long, thick beard. The priest's faint outline gave him a ghostly appearance, yet Marju did not look terrified at all. In fact, he approached the strange figure as if he had known him for thousands of years. The priest put a necklace of light on Marju. The necklace was embedded with sacred information that could not be obtained elsewhere. The priest then vanished in the darkness of the chamber and left Marju alone. Stealthily moving through the great gallery and into the ascending chamber, Marju made his way out of the chambers of the pyramids through another attached chamber where John was waiting. It was close to an hour before Marju returned and he looked different, more radiant, as if charged with light by the pyramids. He walked confidently toward the car and jumped in the backseat, now ready to head back.

Reverend John climbed into the driver's seat and drove off toward Al-Fayum. Upon reaching Al-Fayum, Marju took off without waiting for the car to stop. He climbed the church gate and disappeared within the shadows of the church. John parked his car and proceeded to his room. Marju did not follow.

The next morning, John spotted Marju sitting as usual at the church gate. John rushed through breakfast and sat next to him. This time Marju looked at John and he felt an unusual sensation run down his spine. The more Marju looked at him, the more John began to understand what Marju was trying to tell him. John could not fully comprehend it, but he could make out bits and pieces. He could see in the cat's eyes the shape of the pyramid and its inner sanctum, where the body of a pharaoh lay in a large hollow slab of stone. The images grew sharper as Marju's eyes locked on John's. The intensity of the glare spurred the images into sharp focus. There was the image of a long procession, with a priest at the head of it, going toward a temple. These images were to be repeated over and over again; each time Marju would look toward the horizon, toward the pyramids. A new set of images would be revealed to John, like the life story of the pharaohs, the story of Joseph, and many other images, one after another, in the eyes of Marju.

What was revealed to Raabia was not the same as what Marju revealed to Reverend John Wilson. Regarding the rest of the revelation, John had to wait until he had completed his work. He was content for now that he had established communication with Marju and hopefully, it would lead to something much bigger. Raabia came to play with Marju, and John was excited in telling her that Marju had looked at him for the first time.

"I know," said Raabia before he could finish.

"How do you know?" asked John, perplexed.

"Marju told me," she answered.

"But you just came. How did he tell you so quickly?"

"We have our ways of letting each other know. In fact, when you gave him milk, he told me that he was going to be friends with you and that he would let you into his world, a bit at a time. You were patient and now you need to shed your skin of dogma. Then the secrets of the pyramids will be revealed. The secrets of the inner world will be revealed to you by Mustapha, who will meet you soon and guide you."

"You do know Mustapha, then?" John asked.

"I met him before you did. In fact, I met him many centuries ago while in Basra."

"I saw him in the Garden of Bliss."

"He resides in many places at the same time," said Raabia. "You will find him in the dervish tekke, a prayer house in Cairo. You will meet him soon and he will lead you to a new experience. In the battle we are about to witness, many will die and you will perform the last rites to the dying. By that time, you would have shed your outer skin of dogma and rituals, and begun your inward journey." She took Marju and disappeared down the narrow alleyways. It was the last time he saw them both. They were to disappear from his life completely. John went back to the church, knelt before the cross, said a short prayer, and then read from the Bible:

"Our Father in heaven:
May your name be honored?
May your kingdom come;
May your work be done on earth, as it is in heaven?
Give us today the food we need,
Forgive us the wrongs we have done,
As we forgive the wrong that others have done to us.
Do not bring us to hard testing
But keep us safe from the evil one."

He got up, washed himself, and went out again. This time he wanted to meet an old man with the "inner vision." Supposedly the elderly man could "see" things that others had difficulty understanding. He had the gift of comprehending parables.

Making his way past the marketplace, John tumbled into a dilapidated house where the old man lived. Knocking on his door and being given permission to enter, John noticed that the aged man had very few possessions: a bed, a chair, and a few cooking pots. The man ushered John to sit down in a rickety chair that appeared to be almost as ancient as the man himself. A slight grunt slipped through the old man's closed lips as he, too, took a seat.

"How long have you made people think a little deeper about life?" asked John.

"When I was once in a church, while others contemplated the parables of Jesus, I heard a voice. The voice was that of a young man. He said to me, 'Only a few understand the parables in the divine books and from wise and intelligent prophets. Others will just take them at face value.' Remember, he used the word prophets. And then the voice went on to say, 'Because you have made the effort by sitting and contemplating on the parables, I will open a window of knowledge for you. This window will allow you to see deeper into the parables, so that you may interpret it for your fellow human beings. You dive into the depths of a parable to bring up the pearl within it. This,' he said, 'is my gift to you.' He then told me this gift will cure blindness in people, which has made them go astray, because they have misinterpreted the parables.

"This is the sight he told me to give to the people. It is not the physical sight that I restore; it is the inner sight through which comes true understanding and wisdom," the man explained.

"What is the hidden treasure as stated in the Bible?" John asked.

“God is the hidden treasure. When someone finds the signs of the Divine, this hidden treasure, he hides it from others—he covers it up, because they would not understand this mystery, since they have not reached that level of understanding.”

“Then what is the meaning of ‘sells everything and buys a field’?” John deliberated.

“He gives up his material wealth and uses it to benefit the poor—in this way he buys his way into the kingdom of the Divine. This is the meaning of the parable of the hidden treasure,” said the old man “Most priests do not know how to interpret this; they read out loud the parable in church and let the people figure it out for themselves. Most people are not enlightened.” The aged man pushed his frail body up and shuffled out the door. He stood with his back against John for a moment, breathing in the fresh air.

“You have been given this gift and you are sharing that with others. That’s most noble,” John said, brimming with admiration.

“I have been given this gift and I relate to people who want that understanding.” John grew excited with each word that passed between them, and soon they were deep in discussion of several other parables, like the one about the unfruitful fig tree.

“The parable is all about fertilizing your soul with good deeds and prayers, and the soul will bear fruit—divine fruit—which implies bliss. The soul is in bliss forever, and nothing in this world could harm him with a blissful spirit.” Wisdom poured from the man’s mouth, like honey from the honeycomb. An hour stealthily passed before Reverend

John realized it was time for him to head back to church. He thanked the aged man for his insight.

On his way back to the church, John caught a man stealing bread from a stall and took off running. He thought to himself about the thief representing the devil, and the bread was nourishment for the soul. The incident could be interpreted as the devil that comes and steals the most precious thing that can nourish your soul, this of course being prayers. Those who do not pray, the devil has stolen the man's prayers, just like the thief, and therefore they are left without spiritual nourishment. With that understanding, John felt spiritually enlightened and soon he was whistling his way back to the church.

The next day being Sunday, John attended church for the morning service and led the congregational prayers. After this he told them that this faith was good for them. "You have in your faith the basic ingredients you would need to become wholesome again. Before you were born, you asked that you be born in a faith that teaches love, because you in your previous life did not have much love. You were a violent, hating young man and woman. But then you were given choices in order to correct those wrongs. Now that you have been given what you wanted, and you promised that you would be better men and women, do not stray from that path. Keep cultivating this path, and you will profit much from it. For now, become a good Christian and love humankind."

6
Maqham Al-Khamosh
(A Quiet Place)

"There is a way between voice and presence
Where information flows
In discipline silence it opens
With wandering talk it closes." –Rumi

John wanted to meet Mustapha and, as Raabia informed him, he lived in a dervish colony. So, he decided one day to find out where exactly this colony was hidden. John walked gingerly toward the Tekke, or Khanna, a ritual house of the Mevlevis Dervishes, near the citadel on Shari Siyufiya, an area that was unfamiliar to him.

Going from one alley to another, he nearly got lost in the labyrinth of twisting dead end streets, until he broke down and asked a man who was sitting on his balcony for directions.

"Where is the Khanna?"

"Your heart is your Khanna," the man replied.

"I want to meet Mustapha," Reverend John tried expounding to help the man understand his request.

“The Mustapha of the rose garden resides in your heart,” the man repeated, chewing a bit of tobacco between words.

“I meant Mustapha of Giza, my childhood friend.” He was getting nowhere with this old man.

“Ah, that Mustapha. He is two blocks down the street full of beggars. All are beggars until they have met Mustapha. With love for the beggars, all will meet Mustapha.” Without another word the man slipped into the house he was standing in front of. John caught a glimpse of him again at the window of the house, with a smile on his face, radiating with light. As John walked down the road, he noticed Major Ross looking inside a shop window. Reverend Wilson thought he might as well say hello, in case the major had noticed him through a reflection in the window.

“Good morning, Major Ross. What a surprise to see you here,” said Reverend Wilson accompanied by a warm smile on his face.

“Ah, good morning, Reverend. What a pleasant surprise. What brings you here? Let me guess: your childhood friend, Mustapha, isn’t it?” said Major Ross, raising his eyebrows and creasing his forehead.

“How did you know?”

“Let’s say intuition.”

“More like spying, Major. You have the audacity to break into my room and steal my diary. I thought citizens were free to wander without being followed or harassed,” John retorted, raising his voice in mild irritation.

"No need to get angry, Reverend. We all have our work cut out for us. You have yours and I have mine," said the major.

"Your work involves keeping tabs on people and holding them in cages. My task is to set them free from spiritual and material bondage. My work is nobler than yours," said the reverend tersely.

"Who said so?" the major spat back.

"God desires that all humankind be free of occupation, colonization, slavery, or any other form of economic, cultural, social, or religious oppression. Each one is free to practice his beliefs, associate with whom one pleases without being followed, and keep their own cultural traditions rather than forcefully adopting foreign cultures. Would you like to adopt a foreign culture? If not, why impose your cultural traditions on others? Is it not unreasonable and dictatorial that we should behave in this way and call ourselves civilized? I think it represents the behavior of the uncivilized, not the civilized." Full of frustration, Reverend Wilson brusquely pushed past Major Ross.

Walking down the road full of beggars, he stopped at each beggar and gave him or her something.

Sometimes a coin and other times snacks that he carried in his bag. A voice then came to him. It was a female voice.

"You have done well for yourself by giving something to the beggars. Let me remind you of a story about a miser. A miser died, leaving a hoard of gold to his son. His father came to him in a dream in the form of a mouse that ran frantically all over the house. His eyes filled with tears.

"One day the son asked his father, 'Why was he running about the house like this?' and the father said, 'Who guards my store of gold now that I am dead? Has any thief found the hiding place?' The son answered, 'None has found your gold, Father. Why does your face look like that of a mouse?' asked the son. The father answered, 'Learn from my fate. To haunt the hidden cache forevermore. An anxious mouse that darts across the floor.'" Then the voice immediately blended into the silence.

Walking another two blocks, John found the place he was looking for. He wondered whether he would have found it without any help from the man sitting on his balcony.

As John entered the courtyard of the Khanna, he noticed a cat sitting on the wall. At first, he thought it was Marju, but he was mistaken as he came close to it. Marju has some distinctive marks on his face and body. This cat had two lines running from his forehead to either side of his face. The body had two lines running from either side of his tail all the way down his hind legs. Marju had only one line running from his forehead down the left side of his face. John approached the cat and stroked it. Then he noticed through the corner of his eye that a man had appeared at the entrance of the Khanna.

John turned around and looked at him. He was tall and elegant looking, covered in a black gown, wearing a honey-colored hat.

"I have been waiting for you. I knew you were coming. I am Mustapha," he introduced himself.

"I know a lot about you. How did you know that I was coming?" asked John.

"When the Divine has plans for you, I am made well aware of them," he answered pointedly. "But first I will tell you a story. Once upon a time there was a man who was used to eating lead. Not a day went by when he did not eat lead. Each day people looked at him with astonishment as he passed by their shops. 'Look at that man!' they would exclaim. 'He is so full of lead that he can hardly walk.' Then one day he went for a swim in the river and he never came back. He drowned. The people used to say, 'He took off for another place that suited his character.' But to be honest, he drowned due to the weight of lead inside him in a river full of filth. Do you understand the moral of this story?" he asked.

"No, I don't," Reverend John admitted.

"The moral of the story is this: Being a full participant in this world's greed, lust, and insincerity, you eventually get bloated with sins. This is called eating lead. Your body gets filled with lead and eventually you drown in a river of sins—a filthy place where all humans of base value come here to swim," said Mustapha.

"Where do people who are full of lead eventually end up?" asked Reverend Wilson.

"They do not go anywhere. Their souls stay close to their graves. They are left there and cut off from the Divine's presence. This is itself hell for them. Noah's ark comes and passes by them, but never invites them to board the ark until and unless they repent. Only the sincere ones are given mercy. The rest are left there beside their graves till eternity."

"Isn't there any compassion left to try to give them another chance?"

"They have been given enough chances. The one hundred and forty-four thousand prophets being sent—isn't that enough time for people to modify their behavior, improve themselves, express love for the Divine?" asked Mustapha. "You will understand a little more when you come to the Garden of Bliss. For now, let me show you around this place, and then we will go to a *sema,* where we will sing and dance, so that you may reach the *Maqham* or station where quietness reigns supreme and where colors are made manifest. This is the first of the many stations on the way to the Divine."

As they walked around the Khanna admiring cherry woodwork of the sema hall, the iwan, and the courtyard, Mustapha showed him the room where the dervishes dressed.

"Here, put this on," said Mustapha as he handed Reverend John the garments of the dervish, including a tall honey colored hat.

"Why do you dress like this? Does it signify anything?" asked John.

"Yes, it does. The black robe represents the grave and the tall hat represents the tombstone. Underneath the black robe is the *tannur*, the pleated frock and a jacket called the *destegul*. Once the dance begins, you will remove the black robe, signifying your rise from the grave, and on to a higher plane, which your dance will take you to."

"And what does the green band around your hat signify? I notice I do not have that," John asked curiously.

"The color green has great significance. Suffice it to say, for now, that it is a symbol of my office," Mustapha evasively skirted around the answer.

Then Mustapha left John to get dressed in his new costume as the other dervishes were now coming into the Khanna. The master and disciples all came together in one place to experience a truly memorable event, a once-a-year event, to reach the station of colors.

"Kafirun," said Hasan, one dervish who recently joined the Khanna.

"I am not a Kafirun. I believe in God," said Reverend John.

"You believe in dogma," Hasan corrected him.

Mustapha overheard what Hasan said and later confronted him. "There is no need for this. All are children of God, no matter what they worship."

"It is not what they worship, it is what they believe. They believe that only they will go to heaven, and everyone else is condemned to hell," Hasan argued.

"It is not important what they believe, but what is the truth. The truth according to our way of thinking is that mankind is God's highest creation. And God did not say some people are created higher than others. It is part of their dogma. So, like all dogmas, this one will fall too one day and they will realize that they have been wrong to condemn other faiths. They will regret this and ask for repentance. What good will it do them then? It will be too late. So let them believe in their dogma. Reverend John has come today to participate with us in this sema," said Mustapha.

Hasan apologized to John and the matter was closed. Having changed into the dancing robes, Reverend John entered the main hall of the Khanna. Before entering the hall, he removed his shoes—a sign of leaving the worldly filth out of a sacred place. Here absolute silence reigned, like a graveyard. In this silence floated the essentials of concentration and enlightenment. Convinced of the power of silence, Mustapha nodded and bowed respectively to Reverend John and all the others dervishes as they formed a circle—the circle of the cosmos and the bow of humility and respect. Departing from the usual order, where the music would start and the dervishes would begin the dance, Mustapha had to explain a few things since Reverend John was a newcomer to the ceremony.

"I would like to welcome Reverend John, my childhood friend, to this Khanna. Like the Prophet, this is your *hijr*—a journey that you have chosen to undertake to reach new heights, a place where dogma can never take you."

"Then what will take me there?" asked John quizzically.

"You must have the courage to break free from dogma. It is a barrier that is placed in front of you out of self-interest. Here you will choose for yourself what height you want to reach and eventually you will become the master of your own destiny." Mustapha's words echoed full of wisdom and truth in John's ears, but his comprehension was still so distant.

"What makes human beings so divergent in their understanding of life?"

"There are three types of human beings. The first kind of is the one who is entirely immersed in the material world, seeking to live life to its fullest and enjoy the pleasures that go with it. The second kind includes the ones whose one leg is in this world while the other is in the other world. He straddles both worlds with ease. Within this second group, there are two types. Those that surf the faith, and those that swim in the faith. The third kind involves the ones whose entire thoughts are of the other world. They constantly dive the ocean of the divine looking for pearls. They find this world a poisoned chalice, killing man spiritually by drawing him away from the essential—the matters of the world hereafter. I am now concerned with the third category of humans. Humans cannot comprehend the Divine unless through great sacrifice."

"What kind of sacrifice are we talking about?" asked John.

"Great sacrifice, because divine light is veiled from the humans by seventy thousand curtains of light and darkness. To attain this light takes much effort. It is like walking on a razor blade—an impossible act that would be put most off. To the dervish, this is easy since, when he is enwrapped in his dance, all the worldly sensations are stripped from him, and only the source of light remains firmly fixed in his mind," said Mustapha. "With this you will enter the garden where the souls will recite to you a verse from *The Rose Garden of Mystery*:

'Go sweep out the chamber of your heart (of the worldly filth);

Make it ready to be the dwelling place of the Beloved when you depart out.

He will enter it.

He displays His beauties.'

You recite the divine names there. Then the souls will ask you, 'What are you doing?' Your reply will be, 'I am sweeping the chambers of my heart.' Then the voice will ask you, 'With what?' Your reply: 'With this broom.' The exchange will continue from there. They will ask you what the broom is made up of, and you'll tell them that it consists of only the name of the Divine." John nodded with understanding.

"Then they will say, 'You only know how to sweep the chambers of your heart for one time only. It is the names of the Divine that should fill your heart, then all the filth of this world will make its way out.' The souls will say, 'There are ninety-nine names, or attributes, of the Divine. Each one, when used properly, will clean the heart of all the dirt and filth of this world.' When you begin the dance, you are like a planet circling around the spiritual sun.

"Initially, the spiritual sun energizes you, then you create your own source of energy and you spin around even faster. The intensity of this fluid motion thus adds further energy to your spin, until you spin with even more intensity than before. As your body and soul join in the whirling, you begin to lose yourself in the spiritual sun. You would have made yourselves one with the Divine," said Mustapha.

"Will this dance take me to the Garden of Bliss? I want to see my mother again."

"Of course, it will take you to the Garden of Bliss, and beyond, until seven stations are reached. It takes a lot of energy to cut through seventy thousand curtains of light and darkness. It is no easy feat. At the first station you are basked in the colors of that station and you take on the attributes of those colors, which are made manifest by a light hidden from you, and which you can only know exists because it makes color manifest."

"How many colors are there at this station?" asked John as he considered the depth of the experience.

"Three: green, yellow, and red. Each color is separated from another by ten thousand curtains of darkness, each curtain finer than a human hair. By the time you reach the first station, you would have to traverse through thirty thousand curtains of darkness. Thereafter, forty thousand curtains of different colors, made from the primary three colors, lie between you and the spiritual sun. These curtains are made up of atoms vibrating at a certain frequency, allowing the pure light to enter into its space and it then manifests itself as a color. For each color, there is 'knight' or *Marbub*. This knight is responsible for raising the curtain as you approach it," Mustapha described.

"Who commands this knight to allow or not allow individuals to pass through?" Reverend Wilson sought out his new mentor.

"It is only from the commandment of the Rabb, or Lord, that these knights follow. When light touches a particular curtain, the atoms are in an excited state, a privileged state, in that they have been chosen to receive the pure light. It would be as if a king came to a town and all the folks were given colorful garments to put on. How excited would the townsfolk be when hearing of the king's arrival? Similarly, the atoms are expecting a king—in the form of light—and their new garment is the color the light has chosen to become manifest. Until that happens, colors do not exist."

John scratched his head in reflection. "Is each curtain assigned a particular color to manifest?"

"Yes, each curtain has been assigned to manifest a particular color. The three curtains each manifest colors—red, yellow, and green—from which all the other colors are derived. These three colors reflect themselves upwards in the form of three pillars, which hold the divine throne of pure white light. After having held the throne of the Divine, the colors are then given permission to reflect themselves into the Garden of Bliss where they enter three flowers. Therefore, before your eyes colors are made and colors are assigned to each flower. All other flowers you see around you with colors, other than the prescribed three, are mixtures of colors. When the tempo of the music changes, you traverse through the curtain of darkness until the next change in tempo. You will then advance to a new curtain of color until you reach the chamber of colors." This all struck John as fascinating, but also mystical.

"What if you are stuck at a dark curtain, does it mean you do need to start all over again?" John asked.

"There is something in your life that is hindering your progress. That 'dark' event that takes the form of your dark curtain prevents you from going any further. After you are denied permission to proceed, you need to fast for forty days as a sign of your repentance, after which you can proceed further and if you promise not to repeat any past errors. Once you cross the last dark curtain, you proceed to the chamber of lights, a place where the throne is situated and represents the finale of the dance. During the finale, you will spin faster and faster, circling that shining throne you see in front of you. The spinning motion will continue until you see the throne of light begin to ascend, until it disappears from your sight," exclaimed Mustapha with a breath of delight.

"What if I was to stop in the middle of the dance because I felt dizzy?" asked Reverend Wilson, sounding concerned.

"You haven't prepared yourself well for this. You need to go back to basics. And there is no shame in that," Mustapha comforted.

The dervishes then sat for a few minutes in absolute silence, in remembrance of *zikr*, the divine word. Khidr approached Reverend Wilson. "Come with me; you will do as you are told. Do not question me, and you will be saved from the wind of fate, which is yet to descend upon you. The fate of this world, the bare outlines of which will be made clear to you after you have finished this assignment, will be one of violence and death. You will be protected from it, like a shield, by the fact that you have come here to elevate yourself to a new spiritual height. Now I command you to sail across the river and when you reach the other shore, burn your boat.

"After that you will go to a town nestled a few kilometers from the river and there lives a boy by the name of Haruf. You will go and kill him."

"Killing is not part of my nature," John protested.

"You said you will do exactly as you are told," Khidr emphasized.

"I know, but I did not anticipate this from you."

"I know about things that you do not know," said Khidr. "Now go and do as I asked you to do."

Now Reverend John was beyond perplexed. With tears in his eyes, perspiration draining down his face, and his hands trembling, the sema was about to begin. What was he supposed to do? Run. Here were his instructions, of which he was confused about and yet he had to fulfill them. John had never killed anyone in his life and that he had to go and kill Haruf repulsed him. The fact that Haruf was a little boy disturbed him even more. John got up and left the main hall in a hurry. Mustapha followed closely behind.

"What's the matter?" asked Mustapha.

"Khidr came to me and he told me to go and cross a river. After that, once I had reached the shore, he told me to burn my boat. Then he told me to go to some town and kill a little boy. No reason given," Reverend John said with trepidation.

"He comes to everyone with the same message. Do not take it literally. All he was saying was once you have embarked on a spiritual journey, there should be no going back; no halfhearted attempt to reach salvation. Therefore, the burning of the boat was meant to indicate precisely that. As for the little boy you were supposed to kill, that stood for your ego and passion. You need to kill those two while they are in their infancy. When they are fully grown within you, it causes you to falter and stray from the spiritual path," Mustapha clarified for him.

"I missed the point completely. Why does everything have to be allegories? Why not in plain, simple English?" protested Reverend John.

"Well, it would be too easy, and one man's interpretation would be entirely different from another, since each individual lives in a different context; you apply the context according to your situation. Is that clear?" said Mustapha, emphasizing the word clear.

Mustapha then related a story of a man lost and wandering in the desert. He met a passerby who asked him, "What are you looking for, or are you lost?"

"Yes, I am lost but I am not looking for anything. I have experienced everything in my life there is to experience.

Now I just want to experience nothing. Life does not matter. Do I have to look for something so that life can become meaningful?" the man asked.

"Yes," replied the passerby. "There is only one thing you should be looking for to make life meaningful: love. If you lose love, you lose everything. Life is meaningless without love. You need love and you should start this journey of finding love. Begin to love God's most noble and highest creation—man himself. It is love for one another that nurtures the love of the Rabb to enter your heart. You won't find or cultivate love in the desert," said the passerby. "As Rumi said:

'From love bitterness becomes sweet,
From love copper becomes gold,
From love the dregs become pure,
From love pain becomes medicine,
From love dead becomes alive,
From love the king is made slave.'"

"There is no love left in the world. Love was taken away from the world a long time ago.

All that was left behind was greed and lust for power," the man retorted.

"Look in your heart. That's where love resides. Empty your heart of all the world's filth, and you will discover love hiding in one corner like a scared cat, afraid to show its face," said the passerby.

"So, we have in our group the same man who was lost and wandering in the desert looking for something," Mustapha related. He continued, "And the passerby who he met is the same man sitting outside on a bench. Let's go and meet him." Mustapha led Reverend John outside. There, on the bench in the courtyard, was a man who had just arrived. It was the same man that Reverend John had earlier passed in the narrow alleyway and asked for directions to the Khanna. He knew where John wanted to go, but waited for John to ask for directions.

"Ah, we meet once again," said John to the man.

"Our destinies are tied with a strong twine. I am the man of the desert, and you a wanderer, lost and in need of direction. With a small sign, you can cross the desert. But first you need to be aware of that sign. That sign is no other than Mustapha. You saw those beggars on your way here. They represent in their black clothing an absorption and an eventual discarding of materiality and ignorance around them into a dark hole of void. The vision that remains is that of light," said the man.

"You sit here while we join the sema, after which we will join you once again," said Mustapha to the man. "We will drink some coffee, after which the priest will take leave." Then the group made their way back into the Khanna.

The sound of the *kudum*, the drum, could be heard in the courtyard, and the man had closed his eyes in contemplation as his inner heart beat in slow motion around the "pole of light" within him. The circle of dervishes, now seated, waited for Mustapha and John to join them. Once they both arrived into the main hall, the sound of a *Ney*, a reed flute accompanied by the *kudum,* signaled the start of the peshre—the dance.

John closed his eyes. His mind began to empty itself of all the material thoughts. In his mind's eye he envisioned a circle of light of the dervishes. Then a luminous cross appeared out of nowhere and settled in the middle of the circle. He bent to kiss it. The cross disappeared into the circle of light. John straightened his back. Then the dervishes slapped the floor with their hands. They had arrived at the bridge, which the reverend had arrived earlier when he met his mother. *Khidr* was once again on the bridge. The reverend spotted his mother through the open gate of the garden.

"Mother, mother!" he shouted. "I am back." His mother rushed toward him and met him halfway across the bridge.

"I knew we would meet. Mustapha told me he would bring you here one more time," said his mother.

"Why did you not tell me, since I would not have had all this anxiety ever since we last met?" asked John, protesting.

"I did not want to spoil a surprise for you," said his mother.

"What are we going to do while I am here?" John wanted to know.

"You will see the rest of the garden that you did not have a chance to see last time," she answered.

Mustapha bowed at the rest of the dervishes and walked around the tekke three times followed by the other dervishes. Each time a dervish reached Mustapha's post, they bowed before proceeding in a circle. Reverend John, while circling the tekke, did his customary bow at Mustapha's post. His mother interrupted.

“Bow a little more; he is Mustapha and he will take you around the rose garden if you show a bit more respect.”

So, the next time John passed the post of Mustapha, he bowed until his head touched his knees.

Other dervishes, observing such humility, followed suit. Then each dervish came face-to-face with another and they gracefully bent forward. Mustapha now took his place at the post and the dervishes then removed and dropped their black cloaks. They symbolically discarded their bodies and prepared to return to the source of light. With their left hand on their right shoulders and their right hand on their left shoulders, each dervish approached Mustapha and kissed his right hand. In turn Mustapha kissed their sikke, the honey-colored hat.

With their right palm facing upwards and the left palm downwards, the dervishes began their dance. A flow of energy that enters the body from the higher planes now allowed the dervishes to spin faster and they repeated the sacred word silently. With a slight shift of position, the dervishes left this world of duality of free will and entered the spiritual world with each fluid movement.

“Come with me, this way, and I will first show you the rose garden,” guided John’s mother as she led him through the planted garden of jasmine, begonias, tulips, and finally to the garden of roses. Each variety of flower represented a certain kind being at his or her level of spirituality, the rose being the ultimate, the highest and noblest of all flowers. There, right in front of him, Reverend Wilson, saw as far as his eyes could wander. His eyes enveloped roses of three different colors, the colors that held up the divine throne—red, yellow, and green.

"What a wonderful sight to behold and cherish," John spoke breathlessly. As he continued, all the while muttering to himself, "Perhaps one day I could be here too, if I try hard enough."

Mustapha overheard him and walked toward him.

"You are almost there. A few things that you have to do will assure you of your place here. You see that spot they're clearing, where the yellow roses are? You will be right there," Mustapha assured him.

"I wanted to be with red roses," said Reverend Wilson.

"That takes many generations. Yours is a good start. It is a yellow rose that eventually turns red. It is then taken from here and transplanted among the red roses. The colors of the roses are only a reflection of the light from above—the station of Al-Khamosh. If you understand this concept, you will sooner be able to do noble deeds that the gardener plants you in the red part of the garden," said Mustapha.

"Where are you amongst the red roses?" asked Reverend Wilson.

"I am that rose, fully open and full of fragrance." Mustapha pointed to a wholly blossomed red rose. "I am that same rose that sits in each believer's heart. You, too, can have the rose in your heart if you are a believer."

Then a nightingale flew and perched upon a fully bloomed red rose and began to sing. Melodies that were only meant for the saints and angels began to echo throughout the garden.

"Why are you here?" the reverend asked the nightingale, "You told the hoopoe that the journey to the *Simorg*, the king bird, is too long for you to undertake."

“What drove me here was the love of the rose. Without the rose, that fully bloomed red rose, I am nothing. That rose, which is in everyone’s heart, enjoys a special place in this garden. I love to sing for that rose, my guide, and my destiny. Although I have never met the *Simorgh*, for now at least I am happy to be with the rose,” the bird chirped in response.

“What a wonderful melody you sing; a perfect combination of lute and flute. Only in paradise do you hear such melodies. We are indeed in paradise,” John speculated.

“I am also known by the name Latifa,” said the nightingale.

“You will see the same Latifa in your village, residing in a mud brick dwelling next to the church. Go and seek her and invite her to recite hymns in your church,” said Mustapha.

As Mustapha was speaking, Reverend Wilson looked up and saw the ethereal outlines of a station.

“Is that the station Al-Khamosh?” asked Reverend Wilson.

“Yes, it is. But what is on the outside is also inside you,” the Mustapha continued, “the whole world and the universe around you are also inside you. Make no mistake about it.” As he spoke, and unlike a poker player in a casino, the night revealed its hand—hundreds and thousands of glittering stars appeared all around them, forming a sparkling blanket…

“There, you see how the night shows off its black gown, studded with glittering pearls on its wedding day. Today is your wedding day—symbolically, of course. The day any person can reach the Al-Khamosh is a wedding day for him," Mustapha explained.

A ladder descended, so fine and so beautiful, made of silk and spun with a layer of gold. Words failed John completely. He was dumbfounded.

"Climb," commanded a voice.

"I can't. I am too scared," John rejoined with trepidation.

"Scared of what?"

"Scared that I will fall off," John reasoned.

"You can only fall into the garden below," said the voice. "It is not as big a fall as that of Adam."

Reverend Wilson plucked a remnant of courage from the bottom of his heart and began to climb. It seemed the climb would never end. At last, he reached the station's *darwaza*, a door. He knocked. A voice answered, "Who is there?"

"A humble servant of the high and mighty. Mustapha sent me," John nervously answered.

"With Mustapha's name on your lips, you are a king, able to enter any time. Otherwise, you are only an intruder, fit to be dust," said the voice. The door then opened and John entered.

"There, you see," said the voice. John saw a spherical chamber. As he looked outside, it was the same as the inside. The world and the universe outside were the same as what he saw inside the chamber. Then he remembered what he was told previously—what is outside is also inside. The voice left John alone to explore the expanse of this station. The station began to spin while John stood still.

"How wonderful!" mused Reverend Wilson, and as he spun himself faster, so did the station. Then out of the corner of his eyes, John saw a ray of light enter the chamber. The light began to diffuse itself until a milky glow lit the whole chamber. He felt warm. Then three beams of light of different colors appeared from his left and parked themselves at his feet. As he looked up, he saw a circle of pure white light descend until it was positioned on top of the three colors. Then the three colors—red, green, and yellow—formed a circle around him and began to rotate, while the white circle of light remained still. John brought his hands close to his chest. The lights lost their color and merged into darkness. The circle of pure white light remained, suspended in midair. The rhythm changed. John was once again back in the garden where he noticed the flowers faded into an abyss of nothing, and the circle which was over him in the station now appeared to surround him and spin with him, until there was no distinction between him and the circle of light. Sweat poured down his face, his heart racing with the rush of adrenaline, eyes closed in concentration, feet firmly planted on the ground but moving, he made the exit of the Garden of Bliss, finally arriving facing Mustapha. He humbly bowed before him as the music stopped and the rest of the dervishes stopped spinning.

The spiritual ceremony concluded with the word "Hu," which encompassed all the names of God, while a war ends with a victory speech and a tally of the killings. In this was the difference between those that seek light and those that live in perpetual darkness in this world. These two forces should not exist together side-by-side, but the fact that they do is a total mystery.

"Now, what did you think of that experience?" asked Mustapha.

"Exhilaration," said Reverend Wilson breathlessly.

"Do not let anyone else know about this. They would consider you to be mad and put an end to you," came Mustapha's sharp warning.

"I will give you my word that I will keep all experiences a secret because they are personal. Each individual will experience it differently and therefore no two experiences will be the same," John promised.

Leaving the *Khanna*, the evening had already cast its long shadow. The cat in courtyard was still there, the man had left, the gate was locked, and John asked someone to open it for him. As he entered the street, he noticed the beggars had gone, evening trade was in full swing with hawkers and shop owners shouting at the top of their voices to entice potential shoppers. He wandered in this chaos, his thoughts still as though he were in a Garden of Bliss, and a melancholy, carefree attitude overcame him. He felt one with himself, that he must have abandoned his worries on the doorstep of the *Khanna* as he left. For now, he was a liberated man who had now been convinced of the certainty of life hereafter; he did not have to engage himself in the pettiness of this world, the grandeur of life to come, for he had experienced it for himself.

On the other side of the desert, the Libyan side, the world was preparing for war, commanded to the politicians by the dark forces of the outer world. It was the strength of light of the sema versus the force of darkness of the war.

The politics of the world, with its emblems and symbols of war, eventually bring ruin to those engaged in it.

7
Latifa

Latifa had moved from Helwan to Al-Fayum after a single bullet killed her son. She collected scrap metal from an army base after settling down in Al-Fayum with her maternal uncle, who was not well to do, but was generous enough to help her through this difficult phase in her life. The first thing she did when she arrived in Al-Fayum was plant a rose garden in memory of her son and in the middle of the garden was a fountain in the form of a cross.

"I will plant roses in this garden, and the world will then be like roses—the best there is and whose fragrance the nightingale loves to sing about. I am that nightingale that sings every day in the garden of roses. I will not sleep until I have sung my heart out for that special rose," she told herself as she began to clear the land and make deep furrows to plant the rose bushes. After having cleared a small section of the garden, her uncle came to chat with her.

"Why don't you sing in church? You have such a lovely voice," he complimented.

"The church that I seek is not that made of brick and mortar, but one of immortality," said Latifa. "I could transform any church with my singing, but to transform a closed rose to a fully blossomed one takes many years of singing. You have to practically sing yourself to death. Only after death can we see the fruits of our lifelong labor. Until then, our work is incomplete," said Latifa. Her uncle left after a little while.

Then a voice commanded: "The *Mahbub* commands you to be at the church to welcome the English priest."

Latifa made her way to the church the next day. She stood in the doorway, a lovely lonely figure. Her hair was tied in a bun, her eyes were beautifully shaped, her skin soft and clear like that of Cleopatra, and she was dressed in a long white summer skirt. She waited anxiously, summoned to do so by some voice in the middle of the night.

It was eleven in the morning when the reverend arrived in his long black priestly garb with an iron cross dangling from his neck.

"Been waiting for a long time, have you?" the reverend asked with a beaming smile.

"Not too long. I practiced my singing while waiting for you," Latifa reasoned.

"You were in the Garden of Bliss and I saw you when I started to sing. I was singing for Mustapha when I noticed all the other roses started to bloom and when I stopped singing, the roses were no longer blooming. Mustapha told me to carry on but my voice could not carry me anymore. I had stopped coming back here. It was my son who said to me to come back here and plant a garden of roses just for him. God willing, he will be close to Mustapha in the Garden of Bliss. For now, my life is devoted to this one cause only," she said. They walked together into the church. The reverend tried to persuade her to sing, but to no avail.

“I was commanded by a voice to come to church today,” said Latifa. “I thought you wanted to speak to me.”

“I only wanted to let you know that I may be called to another task that needs attending to,” said the reverend. “While I am gone, I would like you to sing, if not in the church, at least in your garden.”

“You have been asked to go to the war zone. Isn’t that correct?” asked Latifa.

“Yes, the Lord has commanded me to go to the war zone to comfort the dying and bury the dead.”

“It will be a long war and at the end of its history will be made, and you will be pleased with it,” said Latifa. “Go do what you have been commanded to do.”

“While I am gone, promise me that you will sing for the congregation,” the reverend repeated, hoping for affirmation of his request.

“Yes, of course, but in my rose garden,” Latifa agreed.

“Yes, of course, in your rose garden,” John repeated.

So, during Sunday service, Latifa would sing in the garden and her voice would carry into the church to the congregation. Some days there would only be standing room in the church when Latifa was singing in her garden. At times she would sing songs, crying for her beloved son, and the congregation would cry with her; at other times she would sing about the rose, the rose in her heart, and the congregation would burst with joy and laughter. On one of her singing days, the lights in the church suddenly went out, sending panic through worshipers, who proceeded to rush toward the exit. A small beam of natural light coming from a hole in the roof illuminated the cross, bringing the congregation back in droves to the pew. They thought that they experienced a miracle and as such should remain in their places until the miracle was over. The general expectation was that Christ would jump off the cross, open his arms wide, and say, "Here I am; good to be back after a long time."

But it never happened. Having realized that the light illuminating the cross was coming from a hole in the roof, the disappointed worshippers were relieved when the lights went on again. The reverend had not moved from his position and the statue of Christ was still on the cross.

Latifa's fame and glory had spread far and wide. The neighboring villages and even worshippers from Cairo came to Al-Fayum to hear her sing. One day when she was alone in her garden and Reverend Wilson was passing by, he overheard her singing. He stopped to listen to her. He could only make out a few words:

"One day, this land will be free of wrongs,
And I will sing until God grants me my wish,
That day, will be a day of shame,
For those shielded from shame so far."

Reverend Wilson stopped and talked to Latifa. From what she told him, he knew the days of the king's excesses in Egypt were numbered, and that the reverend would be instrumental in bringing it about.

"How will it all happen?" asked the reverend.

"The dance of the dervish will set in motion the events of that day, which will lead to a new beginning. This new beginning will bring an end to the oppression of our people. We will be free," said Latifa.

During her days when Latifa was not singing, she would attend to her uncle's daily chores, including bringing water from the nearby well. This task was most suited for the household donkey, named Maruf. Now, Maruf has been with her uncle's family for some time now. He only needed to be fed once a day and he would attend to his task with great fervor.

One day a teacher, who was Latifa's aunt, asked Latifa whether she could borrow the donkey to transport some books to school. Latifa agreed. The aunt took the donkey to her house and had him loaded with books and started toward the school. One the way, there were a few children playing. One of them asked, "How come you are not riding the donkey, instead you put your books on him?"

"Because that would place me in height above the books. And books contain more knowledge than me; therefore, I have given the books the honor of riding the donkey. While I, an ignorant servant of God, must walk to become humble in the face of all knowledge contained in these books," said the teacher.

"We have never heard such nonsense before," said the children.

"You will never know until you have realized that those that have knowledge are better than those that don't. Those that put their knowledge for the betterment of others are even better than those who don't. Knowledge that comes from within oneself is not a burden, like books on this donkey, but a path to the divine." As the teacher arrived at school, the donkey became exhausted, so the teacher took the load off Maruf's back and let him loose.

"There you go. Since none of the knowledge contained in this book will ever be useful to you, you are free to wander. There are men out there who have the same fate as you, so don't despair; you have plenty of company," said the teacher as he let Maruf off to roam.

The teacher then took the books into the school and placed some in each classroom according to the level of learning and intelligence of each pupil. The teacher realized God does the same thing. He gives divine knowledge and wisdom to those who are ready to receive, each one according to his or her level of intelligence and wisdom. Until that day arrives, one has to build that capacity within oneself to receive that knowledge. Putting that knowledge to good use is the sign of a true believer.

Looking out of the window, Latifa's aunt, the teacher, noticed Reverend Wilson passing by the school.

"Reverend, I want to speak to you," she said as she invited him over to her.

"I will be there soon," shouted the reverend as he made his way through the playground and into the school building. "What did you want to speak to me about?" he asked.

"Well, I am worried about my niece. Recently she has abandoned all other pursuits and tends only to the garden. It is like being possessed," she said, sharing her heartfelt concern.

"When one has seen the rose garden, who would not be possessed?" asked the reverend. "There is no garden like that of bliss. Every day you attend to that garden, it brings you closer to your ultimate wish, which is to be close to the rose of Mustapha. You have to struggle with your passions, overcome them, and remove the chain of passion around your soul that holds you back from realizing the truth. Then you will be lifted and soar like an eagle. All your troubles will then come to an end." Then he continued, "You have been fated, since you are surrounded by knowledge. Aim the arrow of love and knowledge at those eager to receive it. Let the 'donkeys' of the human race wander to pasture, as you will not make an impression upon them. Therefore, there is no use even trying. Remember, the task of imparting love and knowledge is only given to a few. You are the chosen one. Do not waste your opportunity. Latifa, the nightingale of the rose garden, and you, in whom intellect reigns supreme, can work together to bring the congregation back to church," said the reverend, now looking serious with his glasses hanging on the tip of his nose.

"And how do we do that in practical terms?" she asked.

"You can teach children to read and write in your spare time without charging for it. It is the most noble thing to do, and let Latifa teach the children to develop their voice potential," he suggested. "Then, after a while, many children will be able to read, write and sing. We will then have a garden full of Mustaphas and nightingales. Joy and harmony would spread throughout the world!"

Latifa's aunt contemplated the reverend's words, and it took time for everything to congeal and make sense to her. They said goodbye to each other, and the reverend made his way out of the school gate, down the path leading back to the village. As John left the school grounds, he passed a donkey grazing in an overgrown field. Maruf and John's eyes met for a split second then Maruf carried on grazing. The reverend was soon out of sight, and Latifa's aunt finished her work at the school. As she left, she took Maruf by his halter and made her way back to the village. Arriving home, Latifa was singing on top of her lungs. The reverend busied himself with cleaning the church, while Maruf's braying could be heard for miles. How true it is that those with little intellect make the most noise!

8
El-Alamein

Do not seek trouble, turmoil, and bloodshed.
—Rumi

There was disturbance to all sorts of balance—the harmony and equilibrium that existed in the courtyard of the tekke, between the fountain, the plants, the flowers, and the trees. All was being disturbed. This agitation was a reflection of the state above in the station of balance. The fountain stopped working and the plants and trees looked as if life had been sucked out of them. Together it signified that something was about to happen.

The cat no longer came and rested on the wall. The old man, who used to come at least once a week, was nowhere to be seen. Mustapha had led the last sema the week before and even he disappeared among the ordinary folks of Cairo.

High above the station of colors, the seven prophets had gathered. The *Marbubs* of the station of balance were going about contemplating what the Rabb had in store for the world. Like an expectant mother, they were anxious when the birth of something catastrophic would take place, knowing full well that it would. The sound of the nightingale had fallen silent and she had not sung for a few days now, since Mustapha was no longer at the sema.

There was a congruence of free will and predestination for the people on earth, a momentous time. The heavenly witness was called. This witness was the same as that on earth, and was asked whether the coinciding free will and predestination could be moved to give people more chance to coexist in harmony and goodwill.

"They have gone too far with their mischief. They have sown the seeds of their own destruction by their greed and lust for power," proclaimed the witness. "Bring down the dark curtain of war and destruction, so we may cleanse the earth of evildoers."

"What shade of curtain shall we bring down?" asked Marbub. "The darkest of them all, or the first shade, the mildest of all the dark shades?"

"We will go somewhere in the middle, not too dark; otherwise, we will have no life left on earth. Be selective about where you bring down this curtain. Consult the station of balance; if unsure, the station will tell you where you need to bring it with full force, while in other places bring it down with half force. The reason for not using the first shade is that we have used it already for the local wars. This is a serious matter. Most of the world will be engulfed in the flames of war, and this war has no equivalence to past wars," said the witness.

Noah's ark was kept busy bringing the good and pious to the Garden of Bliss before their time, in order to avoid them the pain and suffering. Those who had entered the garden were excited that more of their kind would be joining them soon. For the dwellers of the garden, crowding is celebrated with joy and laughter. For here the "like" meet and exchange "notes" for the journey ahead.

The bells of war were rung in the chambers of *Mahbub*. The Garden of Bliss dwellers heard the bells and were worried for their friends and relatives on earth. Special gatherings were in session. Prayers were uttered and the rose garden lost its bloom. These were catastrophic times necessary to balance the good and the evil in the world.

The politicians exchanged signed documents and embarked warships out to sea. The sea-lanes were being mined. Ports and important buildings were being sandbagged. On the battlefields, big guns opened up on the enemy to "soften" them for the final kill. The beastly nature within man himself had been activated by divine will. Now there was no turning back.

Military vehicles, airplanes, and warships were arriving every day at Alexandria from Malta and the British Isles. The drive to the battlefield some sixty miles from the port of Alexandria was now in full swing. Miles and miles of convoys lined the route to El-Alamein.

Major Ross phoned. John picked up the receiver. Not the best of buddies, Ross needed John to comfort the wounded and bury the dead for the impending war.

"Come quickly and join the front-line troops," urged Ross, his voice hitting a high pitch.

"How quickly is it?" asked the reverend.

"Today, if possible. The war at Al-Alamein will break out any day. Our soldiers have nobody to give them the last rites," said the major, his voice choking with emotion.

"I have to pack. Give me a few hours to see if I can hitch a ride from someone coming to Cairo."

He departed for Cairo on a military vehicle convoy out of Al-Fayum and arrived at the Cairo headquarters of the British Army. The headquarters was at The Shepherd Hotel. He found the major seated at a table surrounded by four empty gin bottles. He was unshaven, and his bloodshot eyes were in a daze. It was apparent that he had not slept for three days. There were men in uniform, spies, and secret agents; Egyptians in suits, fez caps; Europeans in smart suits and ties; and beggars in tatters and smelly outwear.

"I am here, Major," announced the reverend.

"Thanks for coming. Though…though…though you oppose the war, our people still need you," Ross said in drunken stupor. "We will beat that scum…scum for starting this war. We need to finish this quickly. You can then go back to Al-Fayum, to your people," said the Major as he drained his glass of gin and tonic. All around him men in uniform finished their last drink, and the coming and going into the hotel became frantic and desperate. The major was soon called away to overlook some maps.

The reverend put on a military uniform, a helmet, and hung a cross around his neck and waited outside the hotel for a ride.

"Hey, Reverend, you come with us," a man shouted from the truck marked with a giant red cross. The ambulance carried him to the front line. On reaching the front lines, after an hour on the road, John could hear the exchange of shell fire, planes screaming overhead dropping their payloads, and loud explosions from it, and bodies scattered all over the battlefield. Then an explosion threw the reverend clear off the ambulance. As he lay on his stomach in the sand, he kissed the cross around his neck as more shellfire hit the already badly damaged ambulance. Next to the reverend lay the ambulance driver, bruised and burnt. Closer examination revealed that he was dead. The reverend administered the last rites to him. A lizard darted past the dead body and disappeared into a hole in the desert floor. John crawled on his stomach toward the sergeant major. He, too, lay there, shell shocked, looking at the emptiness of the sky. John gave him water, half of which trickled down his face and was swallowed by the thirsty desert sand. The reverend got to his feet as soon the sound of exploding shells subsided. He walked toward the troop carriers and a few tanks, a good fifty meters from him. He stopped at the sound of anguished moaning. He had a first aid bag with him, which he had grabbed before leaving the ambulance. He spilled its contents on the ground. Looking for a filled syringe of morphine, he injected it into the moaning soldier. The soldier stopped moaning after a few minutes. His breathing got shallower and eventually stopped. His face slumped over, leaving a frozen blank stare on his face. The reverend felt dejected.

"Oh my God. When I could save a life, you took it away from me," he cried like a child. John lay there not knowing what to do. More shells plummeted toward him. He had no cover. He lay flat on his stomach and began to inch the last few meters toward the other tanks and carriers. The sand was hot and burnt his hands and the khaki uniform. He crawled a little faster in desperation before the next round of artillery shells were to hit him. One exploded just a few meters from him, sending a blast of sand and other debris toward him. Partly buried in sand, he cried in agony as if badly hurt.

“Oh, my leg, my leg!” he cried.

A soldier ran toward him.

“What’s wrong, Reverend?” he asked.

“My leg. Can you look at my leg, just here, below the knee?” John held his knee and the pain streaked across the lines in his expression.

The soldier looked at and pressed gently. The reverend screamed in agony. The soldier’s hand felt something wet. It was covered with blood. The soldier then ripped his shirt and made a tourniquet and tied it above the wound. In a short while the wound stopped bleeding.

“I saw you run with a first aid bag. Where is it?” the soldier asked in panic.

“I left it a short distance away. Can you see that soldier lying there?” he asked, pointing to the soldier he had just attended to.

“Yes, I can see him.”

“Well, it is next to him.”

The soldier ran in a half-crouched position toward the bag. He looked at the bag. There was one bandage in it, a few morphine ampoules, a splint, and a few bottles of drugs. He could not identify the exact contents, for the markings had been covered with sand. He grabbed the bag and ran toward where the reverend was lying. Having gotten to the reverend, the soldier bandaged him up and carried him. With one arm of the reverend around his shoulder and hopping on his right foot, they made it to the tank area. On reaching the personal carriers, still standing upright despite that barrage of shells, the reverend was made to sit in the back seat with another injured soldier. The hot desert sun sent a stench of rotting bodies and the spillage of rations of canned fish, beef, and beans toward the personal carriers.

"Someone here is in pain. I don't think he will make it in the next few minutes," said a voice. Grabbing a bag of morphine, the soldier who had just dropped off the reverend now attended to yet another dying soldier. He was dead by the time he got to him. The reverend prayed:

"I call the Lord for help;
I pleaded with him.
...Rescue us from our troubles."

Night was falling fast. The flashes of distant artillery shells igniting against the black sky were clearly visible on the horizon. Some men were busy unloading tents, food, and clothing from the carriers. Scorpions, lizards, and rats advanced in brigade numbers as the evening breeze swallowed up the heat of the day. Scattered dead bodies were quickly rounded up and given a decent burial. A wooden cross marked the graves of fallen soldiers. One of the signs read: "Mark Buckingham. Here lies a friend and mentor, taken away before his time."

The next day the relentless air attacks and shelling continued, wounding scores, destroying valuable rations, and wiping out military vehicles. A thousand-pound bomb hit a field hospital, sending John diving for cover. When the raid was over, a number of wounded soldiers were dead. Shortage of bandages, antiseptics, and chloroform made the task even more difficult. Countless lives were lost due to these shortages.

John served both as a rudimentary medic and a priest. Trained in first aid, his help was sought at numerous times when the workload got too much for the nurses and doctors. With a smile on his face and a willing attitude, he was well regarded by the men on the battlefield. In fact, on one occasion he showed enough courage to repel a German attack on the camp. When he was on sentry duty at night, he used to practice his whirling dervish dance, much to the delight of other soldiers and officers, who joined in. It was his way, as he put it, of "maintaining my sanity in a field full of lunatics."

It was during one of his dances that he heard the voice of Latifa.

"Where am I?" asked the reverend.

"You are between the states of the blaming self and the balanced self, where you renounce your worldly desires," said Latifa.

"I have renounced my worldly desires—I have no clothes, the furniture is bare minimum, and I have no car. Doesn't this qualify me to be beyond the balanced self?" asked John.

"Not yet; when you have experienced the station of Mizan is when you have achieved true balance. Until then, you have to struggle," said Latifa. "Each person has to go through seven stages before light dawns in his heart. The first is the compulsive self, dominated by ego, desires, and instincts. Each can conquer this state through prayer, repentance, and remorsefulness. The second and the third state are as I just described to you. The fourth stage is that of tranquility, peace with oneself, the pacified soul. This is the part where one lives on a higher consciousness with constant remembrance, or *dhikr*. It is where the heart finds tranquility. In the fifth stage one finds happiness with Rabb, and there is no questioning about his motives for this or that happening in the world. It is to be accepted with endurance, forgiveness, and gratitude. In the sixth stage you exist side-by-side with God, and you are the agent of Rabb, doing his work. Your existence is one of total humbleness and submission. The seventh stage is that of the perfected self. You and the Rabb are one and the same."

"But I have all those qualities," protested the reverend, "and I am stuck in between the second and the third stage."

"I know it is hard to go through each stage—the war, the suffering, and poverty—without losing patience. But if you endure it with patience, there is a greater prize at the end," she said, full of hope and promise.

"Now I am running out of patience," said the reverend.

"Never run out of patience. It is the worst thing that can happen to you. All that you have attained so far would have been in vain if you do not cultivate patience within yourself. Moreover, you were destined to be here. That means that although you were against the war, you had to come and attend to the dying and in turn you had to witness man's cruelty toward others. From now on you will move up the stages quickly, having experienced all that needs to be experienced at this time in your life. Every event in your life is a learning experience. So don't complain; accept what is destined for you." Latifa left those words with John before departing.

The evening had taken root. The moon was out in its full glory, and the stars played second fiddle to it. The temperature began to fall to freezing point and a campfire was lit, shielded from the prying German eyes by tanks and troop carriers.

"Want some coffee?" Phillip offered. Phillip was a gunner in the regiment and had moved from Mersa Matruh to El-Alamein as a last defensive stand for the allies. Rommel and his men were now just sixty miles from Alexandra as panic struck the residents of Cairo and Alexandra and many had fled the cities in droves.

"Yes, I wouldn't mind some. The desert air is chilly out here," said the reverend, taking a cup of coffee from Phillip and pulling his coat closer to enclose his body heat.

"You know, I was in Cairo just a few months ago, and I read in the papers that a person by the name of Hassan had been arrested together with other officers. They found a shortwave radio and maps of military installations, and a few thousand paper bills. The article said that Hassan was an air force officer and also a whirling dervish. Do you know whom I am talking about?" he asked. "Since you are engaged in this whirling dance you should be familiar with your fraternity."

"There are many Hassans in Cairo. There is one I know whom I met at a sema. I did not know what his last name was. If it is that Hassan, I did not know he was an officer in the Egyptian Air Force," John replied incredulously.

"In Al-Fayum they arrested Abbas. They also found on him a shortwave radio and codes for communicating with a German spy," Phillip added candidly.

Abbas was Latifa's uncle, and John was surprised that he was involved in anti-British activities. For he knew Hasan was opposed to foreigners, with the incident John experienced at the sema, but Abbas was a complete dark horse. Maybe he got involved in this after John left Al-Fayum for Alamein, or perhaps at the prompting of Latifa. Did Latifa somehow know that Hasan was involved? Was it Hasan who was communicating with Latifa, or on the other hand, was it Mustapha acting through Hasan? All these questions perplexed John as he embarked on a journey to find the truth. But first he had to see the war through.

It was 8:00 p.m. London time on the 23rd of October, when Churchill received a coded signal from General Alexander in Cairo that "Operation Lightfoot" had begun. For the past twenty-four hours, the allies had moved men into deep trenches, concealing them from the German and Italian reconnaissance flights. Men were ordered to sleep and eat in the trenches, three foot by six sweltering graves, until the orders came to attack the enemy. At the destined hour, one thousand guns opened up on the enemy. The night had turned into daylight, like a white coffin sheet of light spread over the battlefield. One German soldier wrote: "The peaceful stars were shaken in their heavens."

Advancing toward the enemy, many fell from the exploding mines laid carefully hidden in the sand and artillery barrage that opened up from the opposite side.

The reverend, now well behind the tank positions, was told to make quick runs to get to the wounded. Finding wounded men and under constant shellfire, the reverend found it the most difficult task he ever had to accomplish. The ambulances he had ordered got stuck in the soft sand, while others that managed to reach the reverend had their tires blown off when they hit a landmine. The wounded lay there, helpless, unable to reach any field hospital. Many died due to lack of care. Others had to have their legs or arms amputated when gangrene set in. To add to the misery, the rains came, turning the desert into one soggy mess. Men and machines crawled to a slow pace. Soldiers, tired from being without any sleep for three to four days in a row, now found their energies further sapped by having to move heavy machinery through wet, soggy sand. Supply lines were stretched, ammunition and food was running low, and winter gales caused havoc with the ships in the Libyan harbors.

The German army was threatened from the west by the arrival of the Americans, who had landed in Morocco and Algeria. They brought with them tanks, paratroopers, and fresh supplies. The paratroopers were dropped at the oasis town of Gafsa, which they captured easily from the German defenders and then went on to hold the flat land between the two Atlas Mountain ranges. The final push came when Alexander, commander of the Anglo-American forces, made his way to the coastal city of Bizerta, where the German forces had to withdraw. Then Tunis fell to the allies and forty thousand Germans surrendered. This was the beginning of the end of the war, whose final phase began at El-Alamein.

Defeated German and Italian soldiers were seen with their hands raised marching in a single column toward the prisoners of war camp. The battle of El-Alamein had ended like it began—by the will and command of the *Rabb* of all worlds.

John made his way back to Cairo from the battlefield, his services no longer required. Upon arriving in Cairo, he went straight to the army headquarters at The Shepherd

Hotel. There Major Ross was celebrating with other soldiers over the allied victory at Al-Alamein.

"I am here to find out where you are holding Hasan and Abbas," John said to Major Ross.

"Ah, Reverend, you are back from the field," Ross replied, ignoring the request. "How was it? Must have seen some awful things happening out there."

"Yes, awful, gory things happen in war. I am so disgusted with it all that I warned you previously that we are paying for our voracity and our insincerity. And we did pay a price, didn't we?" asked the reverend passionately.

"But we won, didn't we? What are a few hundred thousand men dead?" the major brutally retorted.

"You have no respect for humanity, do you? Including your own people?"

"I have no time for emotional outbursts. Regarding the two arrested spies of yours, they are in the Cairo prison. You can go see them whenever you wish. Give my name and they will let you through."

The reverend took a cab to the prison, a sprawling compound with tents surrounded by barbed wire.

"I have come to see Hasan and Abbas. Major Ross said I could see them," said the reverend to the armed guard.

"Follow me."

Leading the way through a narrow path past some cabins, there against the barbed wire stood Hasan and Abbas. Both had bleeding cuts.

"It is good to see you, Reverend," said Hasan.

"Good day, Reverend," said Abbas.

"Good to see both of you. What's happened to your hands?" asked the reverend.

"Oh, well, hazards of the barbed wire. Nothing to worry about," said Hasan.

The midday sun was now at its fiercest.

"I heard they found a radio in your possession," said the reverend.

"Well, it was nothing. Some Germans gave it to us. He said keep it so that we could listen to the war news," said Abbas.

"I wanted to help the Germans, since the British have taken over our land, stolen our cultural assets, treated us badly, and imposed hardship on us through this war," Hasan hissed.

"But you knew sooner or later you would be discovered trying to help the enemy. That is treason. You are lucky to be alive," said the reverend. "I am working on the loss of cultural assets, and soon we will have resolution to this matter. Regarding being treated badly, I will take it up with the high command and see if we can find the people responsible for this. About the war, I am also opposed to the war, but I did my duty when called upon to comfort the wounded and bury the dead." Sweat poured down his forehead, and he brushed his hand to wipe the sweat off. "Now that the war is over, there is no reason to hold you in custody. I will see what I can do," John said as he hastily departed the prison compound.

The reverend used his influence through the General Synod in London and the foreign office to have the men released. The General Synod wrote back to John saying that the Defense Ministry opposed release of prisoners suspected as German collaborators.

A few days had passed since arriving from the war front. The reverend began to think in his room. Now that the war was over, he had done his duty to the dying and to his congregation. It was now time to concentrate this last part of his life to the enlightenment as shown by Mustapha. He made his way down into the foyer of the hotel. Omar was still there at the reception desk. A few women, mixed with officers, were chatting at the front door as John made his way out of the hotel to the sema. He knew what he had to do.

9
The Station of Balance (Maqham Al-Mizan)

This station of balance, or mizan, located above that of the station of colors in the deeper recess of the human heart, determines how out of balance the human spirit is. The human heart is where Mary, the mother of Jesus, resides. It can only be reached with zikr, an evocation of the most glorious names, which acts as a pail drawing nourishment from the heart. Once the nourishment is brought up, the *Marbub* is able to use this as sustenance to penetrate the thick curtains of darkness that come between oneself and the station of *mizan.*

Previously when the reverend was at the end of a sema, he approached the station with the word "Hu" on his lips, a rose in one hand, and the nightingale on his shoulder. While Latifa sang the sweetest melodies that immeasurably pleased the angels, the reverend kept on repeating the word "Hu" as he knocked on the darwaza.

"I have come with the rose of Mustapha in my hand and the nightingale on my shoulder. Am I allowed to enter?" the reverend meekly asked. A voice answered. It was that of *Marbub*.

"But you have to answer a few questions first. It will show me whether you are ready to enter the station of *mizan.* What can you tell me about the station of colors that you had just visited?"

"What a sight I witnessed! The ladder was made of finest strands of gold and silk. The station spun while I stood still. I saw the throne of pure white light of the divine being held aloft by the red, green, and yellow light."

"What can you tell me about the colors? What do they symbolize?" asked Marbub as he changed his garment, which now reflected the light red.

"The color red represents the sign of gnosis—mystical gnosis. It is a kernel of a seed, like the mysteries embedded in the kernel of the *Rabb*, and those who are thoroughly immersed in the 'sea of the divine' only know a seed. Your garb is a reflection of that color," said the reverend.

"Then who is authorized to possess this gnosis?" asked Marbub.

"First, the *Rabb* has to designate who wears such a garment. It is a garment not easily given to anyone, except to those who hold the balance in their right hand, and the balance does not tilt one way or another. In other words, the balance's pointer, which takes its instruction from 'spiritual pole,' is dead center, and is therefore given to wear such a garment. An individual, and there is only one designated for this world, is the perfect man. Everyone should follow this perfect man if he or she wishes to get anywhere up the spiritual ladder.

"Then there is the color green. It is the color of the pacified soul. It is this color through which the angels ascend and descend into one's heart, bringing compassion and love into one's heart," explained the reverend.

"So far so good," Marbub answered. "What is the yellow color for?" he asked.

"The yellow color stands for the world of the spirit, the world where angels dwell, who at the command of the Rabb are able to ascend and descend to and from the terrestrial world. This is when the humans make contact with the other world through the medium of angels," said the reverend. "It is the same place in the Garden of Bliss where the yellow roses grow."

"We now come to the station of mizan, or balance. Here your every action is weighed and recorded. This station has many 'rooms,' and each 'room' has a scale, and each scale for a different task. For example, to place your intellect on a scale you need to go to a particular 'room,' and to weigh the soul you would need a different scale in another room. Then there is a mizan to weigh numbers and letters. Each letter and number is assigned a particular 'weight' according to its worth. The sacred numbers and letters are assigned a heavier weight than all others. There are the balances that measure the degree of excellence in geometry of shapes in architecture, the material world, and the vegetative world," said Marbub. "These worlds are then able to communicate with each other only when they are in balance. Then with each cycle of time that is between creation and destruction everything is then rebalanced for the new cycle.

"This is the 'chamber' where letters take shape," continued Marbub. "You see that there are only two letters on the wall. These two letters, called *alif* and *ba,* are the most important letters you will come across. Alif symbolizes the origin of all that you see and don't see around you and beyond. *Ba* represents the first intelligence, or intellect. In fact, one can say that the first thing that God created was the intellect when he said 'be' and the worlds were formed. Let's see what's in the next 'chamber.'"

When the reverend arrived in the next chamber, he was a witness to the balance of numbers. Here the calculation was performed by adding the different worlds—that is, the world of knowledge, will, and souls together with man—and one arrived at a sum total of nineteen, representing the levels of hell or of paradise. It also represents the number of angels guarding the entrances to heaven or the horsemen at the entrance of hell. Man is capable of ascending or descending to these worlds at any time in their lives. Therefore, these two worlds are balanced if they were ever to exist side-by-side.

"Would you like to touch the number nineteen?" asked *Marbub.*

"Yes," said the reverend.

As soon as he touched the number nineteen, the gates of hell and heaven opened right in front of his eyes. At first, he was terrified. The nineteen henchmen of hell came toward him with great speed. He wanted to step aside but could not. He was frozen with fear. The nineteen angels then appeared to cut off the path of the advancing henchmen. For now, he was saved, but it was a close call. With his hands and his forehead covered in profuse sweating, John was trembling.

"Not to worry. They would not have come for you," said *Marbub*. "It was only a demonstration. You were saved by the intervention of the perfect men, who balance heaven and hell in each individual."

The reverend was next led to an area where the number twenty-eight was being balanced.

"There are twenty-eight prophets being mentioned in the divine book. Each prophet brought the divine law, perfectly balanced for the people of those times and with their level of understanding," said *Marbub*. He added, "Each law is balanced so that an individual can decide to what degree he will follow the law. There is a leeway allowed for an individual to be tailored to his or her self's external environment in which they live. Some environments can be constrained and therefore the Rabb has made allowance for this. In other words, the law is flexible enough to be applied at any epoch.

"There is geometry through which the personality and character of each number is expressed in the universe. For example, the number zero represents the divine essence, while the number one would represent the creator, since he is the one and only. In terms of geometry, it is represented by a dot. The number two is represented by two dots joined by a straight line. This represents the intellect. It is the intellect which was created first, but it is given a number two position after that of the creator. The number three, represented by a triangle, is the soul. While the number four, a square, is representative of matter. I will now take you back to the Garden of Bliss to explain to you how the garden is laid out in geometrical shape so you understand it much better."

Next, they went to the Garden of Bliss.

"Open," *Marbub* commanded. The gate opened. "Come this way," he instructed, leading the reverend through the garden. "You see the garden itself. It has both the centrifugal force within it and a centripetal force. As you enter the garden, the centrifugal force picks you up and drives you increasingly to the outside and keeps you on the outside. This is the place from which you experience paradise. But paradise is not enough. You should try to get to the center. That is where the essence is. Your determination will eventually drive you toward the center, the spiritual center, where you will find the fountain. The centripetal forces take over and drive you increasingly toward the center or the fountain."

Now that he had seen the station of balance with its multiple chambers, and how the Garden of Bliss was laid out, the reverend was able to get just a small glimpse of the workings of the universe.

The kudum had stopped beating, the *sema* was now over, and the reverend faced Mustapha and bowed. All other dervishes did the same, and bowed toward each other as a mark of respect.

As soon as the reverend left the sema hall, out in the courtyard appeared the man sitting on a bench.

"Which part of the tour did you enjoy the most?" he asked.

"The balance of letters," said the reverend.

"Why?"

"Because without the letters A (alif) and B (ba), the universe would not have been created."

"You have grasped the essentials, which few are able to comprehend. From now on, you will be able to initiate events in this world, which will have far greater consequences than you will ever realize," the man pronounced upon him. The cat that was sitting on the wall now jumped down and sat near the man.

"He knows what I am saying," the man said, pointing to the cat. "He understands me perfectly."

"I can see that. Is he the same cat, Marju in Al-Fayum?"

"He is the same cat, but his features have been changed slightly so that you would not be able to recognize him as Marju."

The reverend took leave of the old man and made his way out of the wrought iron gate into the main street. Here he saw Major Ross again.

"Oh no. It's you again. You seem to hang around like a bad smell," said the reverend angrily.

"How was the meeting there?" Major Ross asked skeptically. "You know, I will have to report to the General Synod Council that you are practicing some mumbo jumbo faith, and that you are acquainting yourself with some nasty elements who want to reduce our influence in Egypt," the mayor threatened.

"You mean, they want to reduce your thievery of their cultural assets and exploitation of the Egyptian masses. Go ahead and report me. After what I have seen today in there, I have no fear left in this world." With that said, the reverend briskly walked away from the major, who ran after him.

"You know, I can deport you from Egypt. You will never be allowed to come back again!" Major Ross screamed at Reverend Wilson's back. John flew around to face him.

"Be my guest. What is about to happen in the coming days does not require me to be here. It will happen with or without me. I have seen the future."

"Nothing will happen. The British will rule Egypt for some time to come, whether you like it or not."

A black limousine pulled up and the major climbed into it. The driver drove off, kicking up enough dust to cause the reverend to cough.

"The world could well do without the likes of him," the reverend muttered to himself as he made his way down the narrow streets, stopping to buy some fruit from the street vendors. He would be glad if he never had to see Major Ross again.

10
The Verdict

The investigation in London, arising from the murder of Reverend Locke, examined the connection between the murderer and the various antique dealers. The detectives in charge replayed the interview conducted on Mrs. Johnston, the murderer, and one of the antique dealers by the name of Alfred Fenton. They attempted to establish a connection between the two. Both were from the same town in Yorkshire, grew up together, and went to school together. But that's where the affiliation ended. After that, both parted ways and were not in touch. The trail went cold. Finally, there was a break in the case. After a few days of not getting anywhere, the detective decided to search Mrs. Johnston's apartment. When her apartment was searched, the detective found a receipt of a holiday camp that she had stayed at during the early forties. Talking to the management of the camp, it was found that Mrs. Johnston made friends with a few guests. The inquiry now focused on her acquaintances at the camp and on her neighbors in a small Yorkshire town.

Detectives fanned out across the country trying to trace relatives and acquaintances. Some had died, and others had moved overseas, who needed to be contacted, thus the case took a little longer to solve. One relative who lived in Leicester was called "Betsy," a nickname given to her by Mrs. Elaine Johnston. She said that Elaine had an aloof personality and had married a man while in the psychiatric hospital who went by the name of Alfie. Further inquiries determined that Alfie had arrived from Birmingham and was in a room next to Mrs. Johnston at the hospital. The detective who was taking notes, Sergeant Pete Howe, was from Birmingham, and he pursued the inquiry with Superintendent Nick Knowles of the Birmingham police.

"Is this Superintendent Knowles?" asked Sergeant Howe.

"Yes, speaking," replied Knowles.

"We have a murder case in London, and I wonder whether you can follow-up on Alfie, a short name, I presume, for Alfred. We don't have his last name. It seems he was admitted to Leicester General Hospital's psychiatric ward in 1942, and is from Birmingham. Further details are not available, and we will let you know if anything new comes up on this person."

"Have you gone to see the hospital staff at the Leicester General?" asked the superintendent.

"We are on our way. In the meantime, see what you can find," Sergeant Howe instructed.

At the Leicester General Hospital, the administrative staff brought the old records out and found that Alfie was none other than the antique dealer, Alfred Fenton. Reports from Birmingham stated the same. In fact, Alfred's father was an antique dealer in Birmingham who was posted abroad in the Far East during the Burma campaign. Now the puzzle began to make sense to Sergeant Howe. Mrs. Johnston had married Alfred Fenton in Leicester. Both had moved to London and lived in the Kings Road area. Alfred ran an antique shop right across the east India Docks in London, where merchant ships from around the globe docked, bringing merchandise to England. It looked like Alfred was involved in a smuggling operation, bringing in antiques from Egypt and the Far East. As to the different last name, it was found out that in the marriage registry records she had decided to keep her maiden name. Questioning Mrs. Johnston any further was unwarranted.

Meanwhile, in Egypt the police were following up on the investigation in London. They wanted to know what the connection was, if any at all, between Sid Carter, Alfred Fenton, and Mrs. Johnston. Records were searched at the offices and warehouses of the Egyptians Date Company, the Suez steamship company, and the Ministry of Antiquities. Boxes and boxes of documents were carted away to police headquarters. Police in London were asked by the Egyptian police to look into a warehouse at the east India docks, where Sid Carter had a clearing agent working there. Also, they were asked to look at the country house in Kent, which belonged to Sid Carter, and where he stayed whenever he visited England. Besides Sid Carter, there was also a cabinet minister under suspicion, whose links to the king were to be explored, since the king and his ministers all had ownership in a number of companies based in Geneva.

It took a while for the whole investigation to be wrapped up. It dragged on for over one year. When it was finished, summons were issued for Sid Carter, a cabinet minister, an official of the Steamship Company, a number of employees of the Ministry of Antiquities, Omar, the receptionist at the hotel, where the reverend stayed, and surprisingly Major Ross. The army had protested this at the highest level, but the magistrate declined to absolve him of further questioning. The army was afraid the link between the ministry of defense and the antique dealers would be become well-known, and through the ministry others links could be exposed that would be embarrassing for the government, who was always protesting about the inside corruption, and here was a prime example of hypocrisy, a widely known attribute of the occupying power.

The investigating magistrate from the temple bar was middle-aged, wore baggy trousers with an untucked shirt exposing a half wrapped red gown, and whose teeth looked like a set of piano keys. The rumor was that when he was a child, his mother used to force him to play the piano, despite his hatred of it. One day at school, he remarked how his mother had rammed the piano down his throat when he told her he was sick of playing the piano. One of his friends then remarked that his teeth looked bad because of his mother constantly ramming the piano down his throat, and that some of the keys had got stuck in his mouth.

The prosecuting lawyer, wrapped in a black gown, had his shiny gray hair standing up on end. He wore a shocking pink tie, white socks and shirt, with black pants.

As the questioning continued, the annoying flies, now large and bloated from gorging on a nearby garbage dump, were moving between the magistrate to Sid Carter, who whisked them away with his hands. The magistrate had a fly swatter, which he used effectively, killing a dozen of them with one swipe of it. A few flies got stuck in the prosecutor's sticky Brylcreem laden hair, and struggled to free themselves. The overhead fan was ineffective in keeping the courthouse lukewarm. Extra fans were brought in, but the situation got no better. The assembled public used newspapers, handkerchiefs, and handheld fans to cool themselves. The temperature rose to uncomfortable levels. Everyone was glistening with sweat and some who had fainted were put in an ambulance and whisked away to the nearest hospital.

Sid Carter, acting for himself as defense attorney, trapped the prosecutor many times in his own greasy arguments of whether there was a conspiracy to export artifacts, or just a simple case of greed. As more flies got trapped in his greasy hair, he asked the magistrate for an adjournment. The magistrate haphazardly received an earful of a strong defense argument from Sid accusing the prosecutor of wasting time, adding that his justice was at stake if the proceedings were delayed. The magistrate, a paid servant of the government, had no choice but to take the prosecutor's side and grant an adjournment, knowing full well that not to do otherwise would involve risking his job and thereby his pension. Leaving the courtroom through the back exit, the magistrate retired to his chambers, pulled out a bottle of whisky from his desk drawer, and drowned himself in it.

On resumption of the proceedings, arguments between the prosecutor and defense volleyed back and forth. John's cross, dangling from his neck, was a sure visible sign of the presence of Christ in the courtroom. It prevented the obvious lies and swearing that often-accompanied trials of greed, fraud, and corruption. The reverend was called as a prosecution witness.

"Name?" asked the prosecutor.

"Reverend John Wilson."

The magistrate, now falling asleep, straightened himself. Pushing his glasses up his nose, he took a good look at the reverend. "Do you recognize this man?" asked the prosecutor.

"Yes, I do. He is Sid Carter," answered the reverend.

"What do you know about the artifact smuggling operation?" the prosecutor pressed.

"Well, as far as I can tell, there are a few people involved, according to London police," answered the reverend.

"Do you see those individuals here in court?" asked the prosecutor.

"Yes, sitting with the defense," answered the reverend.

"What about Sid Carter, who is conducting his own defense? Is he involved as well?" asked the prosecutor.

"As far I can tell, the warehouse he owns is a staging area for the artifacts before leaving for Europe," replied the reverend.

"What proof do you have?"

"There are a few of my parishioners who work there and they believe that the markings on the crates are special codes to indicate artifacts in them," replied John.

"That will be all at this stage," concluded the prosecutor as the reverend stepped off the bench.

Then prosecution hammered the point that Sid, having lived and owned a business in Egypt, should have prevented him from engaging in such behavior as artifact trafficking.

Sid Carter looked at the prosecutor with the eyes of naivety, the argument of course falling on deaf ears and a heart hard as stone.

The police report from London was presented, the psychiatric assessment of all involved was presented, and the entire network of dealers and agents was exposed. The magistrate was so impressed with the prosecution team that he recommended that the entire team be granted a permanent civil servant status. This brought laughter from the courthouse. Embarrassed at this gaffe, the magistrate stood up to indicate the end of proceedings for the day, and the adjournment of the court soon followed and he retired to his chambers.

There was a rush for the exit and two elderly ladies who came to court for some juicy gossip were jostled and manhandled. The lone policeman on duty was now made to feel utterly useless. He sat down on a bench thoroughly disgusted. John, with prayer beads in his hands and the obvious cross hanging from his neck, was not given any priestly treatment either. In fact, he was relegated to the end of the scrum, where he and the prosecutor had a small chat on their way out. A few reporters wanted to talk to the reverend and he obliged willingly.

"Just a few questions, Reverend," asked one reporter.

"I will take two questions only," replied John.

"My first question is how does it feel to have contributed to the breakup of this smuggling operation?" asked the reporter.

"Just a small contribution to the well-being of the country," replied John.

"What are your plans now?" asked the reporter.

"To stay around till the end," replied John. He then left the reporter who was busy making notes.

The next few days, the magistrate would visit each prisoner in the cell. These prisoners were the dredge of the society—poor and ignored—and were locked up because they could not afford bail money. The justice system, which had favored the rich and the powerful, were granted bail, even if they were suspected of absconding bail and fleeing the country. The jail itself was no picnic for prisoners. In fact, it was crawling with all sorts of insects, including the dreaded red spider, whose sting would smother any hope of seeing the next day's sunrise. Then there were the lice in blankets, blood sucking, thirsty for human blood, and the ants, an army of them that formed a long queue from the latrine to the cell door. Some prisoners thought it was the British training that enabled the ants to form a queue. The prisoners were of the variegated kind—prostitutes locked up with petty thieves, deserters, and hardened criminals. The place was stinking with unkempt prisoners sweating in the sweltering heat, with no ceiling fan to provide any relief. Half of them were stripped down to their waist, and the other half were unclothed from their waist down. A cacophony of sounds emerged from the prison, which could be heard for at least fifty meters from the prison gates. As more prisoners arrived, the jail was bursting at its seams and it added to the stink and the noise. The judge, having made a note of the atrocious conditions, threatened to free all prisoners if the government did not improve conditions immediately. He did not want to see, if ever convicted, the rich and powerful Sid Carter ending up in this sorry place.

The following morning a crew of cleaners arrived with bleach and brooms and thoroughly cleaned the place up, leaving a fresh smell emerging from it that made the judge so satisfied that he tore up the threat. Overcrowding was further relieved when a disused wing was repaired and a few prisoners, mainly small-time thieves, were transferred out.

One day, while the trial was still going on, Mustapha made a grand entrance and the proceeding came to a halt as everyone present in the courthouse turned around to watch the tall majestic figure take his place in the visitor's gallery. He was there to observe the true course of justice as it related to the case of the Egyptian Date Company. The judge was most interested in the code marking on the crates, and asked the prosecutor to invite someone well versed in deciphering the secret codes on the date crates. The problem being of a mathematical nature, the prosecutor thought it prudent to give the task to a university professor. He went to see Professor Ghalib of Cairo University, who sat disinterested as he heard the prosecutor outline the problem. The professor made no commitment that he would be able to solve it, but that he should be given a few weeks at least to come up with an answer. He did come up with an answer in just one and half weeks. The magistrate sat listening to the professor outline how the various numbers fall into a certain pattern called the Fibonacci theory of numbers. Scores of crates were brought in as he outlined for the jury how the number pattern fit flawlessly with the said theory and how the code on crates used a number theory to locate which crates contained the artifacts and which contained only the dates. Then there was the question of the marking "x" on some crates while others simply displayed plain numbers. This was solved when the prosecutor offered some crates that he had pulled out of the warehouse to demonstrate the number theory. He said that those crates marked with an "x" had more valuable artifacts than those marked without an "x." The valuable cargo was destined for an agent at the London dockyard where only special antique dealers, with over two or three million pounds in sales every year, were permitted access to such crates. The magistrate then asked a few questions that troubled him.

"Then who do you think is knowledgeable in the science of mathematics within the Egyptian Date Company to think of a brilliant idea to codify the crates with Fibonacci numbers? That needs to be proved before I can accept the link between The Egyptian Date Company and the nature of the content of the crates in accordance with the marking on the crates," said the magistrate gruffly.

The prosecution now had a problem on its hands: proving someone inside the data company had knowledge of Fibonacci numbers and used that knowledge to stamp markings on the crates. The prosecution case could be furthered if he struck a deal with an antique dealer for an offer of leniency. The weakest link in the antique dealers' chain was a man named Henry. He was a French national who had settled in England and recently got involved in the antique business. Approached with an offer of a fine of fifty thousand pounds over jail time, he was requested to tell the court who trained him in recognizing which crates contained artifacts and which only contained dates. Bringing Henry before the court was an easy task, since he had agreed to cooperate. But the problem lay in his ability to convince the jury of the link, since his English was of a poor quality. The risk was taken to put him on the witness stand. Simple questions were put to him, so as not to unnerve him. He responded splendidly to those questions. Henry said that a person by the name of Omar, whom he had once met in Cairo, was the one who taught him how to recognize the crates with their markings. Now the case was gaining momentum as the magistrate sat back in his chair and listened most attentively. The prosecutor rose to point out an errant question from the defense, but the magistrate waved it off with his hand to dismiss it and allowed the defense to conduct a thorough cross-examination of the prosecution's witness.

"And do you see the man you claim to be Omar here in the courtroom?" asked the prosecutor in a firm but gentle voice.

"Yes, I do," Henry fervently agreed with a nod. "He is right there, the man in the white suit." His long finger pointed to a man sitting behind the defense lawyer.

"That's all for now," said the prosecutor as he sat down feeling well satisfied at having found the missing link in the case.

It was now time to call one of the prime suspects: Omar, the reception clerk at the hotel where Reverend Wilson had checked in on the day of his arrival in Cairo. His time on the stand was only a few hours, as he acknowledged his role in the training of agents in the recognition of the crates. He related how he had studied mathematics under Professor Ghalib and that he had difficulty getting a job at the university, and therefore ended up in the hotel trade. The prosecutor then outlined how some of the ministers were involved together with the king.

The last day of the trial saw also the presence of Latifa, as she sat observing the proceedings. The eye contact between her and the magistrate were a continuous source of wonderment to the defense. Was there an exchange of thoughts between the magistrate and Latifa that could imply a much bigger ring than the prosecutor had managed to net so far? The magistrate was not satisfied with those who were present before him. He wanted additional answers from the prosecutor.

"How is the king involved in all this, since you have outlined the role played by the minister and how he operated a joint account with the king?" asked the magistrate.

"We don't know for sure, due to the secrecy of the banks and their relationships with their clients," the prosecutor faltered. The magistrate looked at Latifa. Latifa had a question on her mind that she wanted an answer to. The magistrate somehow read her mind and asked the same question.

"If the king is not involved, would he not have fired his minister knowing full well that the country's treasures are being carted off abroad while he is the sole protector of all the values, customs, and traditions of this country?"

"We can only speculate, and speculation is not what the courts are about," reminded the prosecutor. "There is no proof that the king benefited, as far as we can tell. The fact the king has not sacked his minister is a cause of concern for us. But the people are the judge of that." The prosecutor took his seat and allowed the magistrate to sum up for the jury. Latifa had other thoughts going on in her head. She did not wait for the jury to arrive at a verdict before leaving the courthouse to return to Al-Fayum.

How many of the ministers were involved, no one would be able to find out. But one thing was sure: corruption needed to be pulled up by its roots; otherwise, society would rot from within and that was unacceptable to most decent people.

The magistrate read the charges out and instructed the jury, who retired in the back room deliberating. After a few hours of debate, the verdict was announced.

"Guilty," declared the spokesperson for the jury. The magistrate retired to his chambers to consider the sentence.

"Ten years in prison for Sid Carter of the Egyptian Date Company, Omar of the Desert Inn, and James Tanner of the British Steamship Company. Five years for Saha of the Egyptian Museum and Ministry of Antiquities. The case against Major Ross is dismissed. There is not enough evidence to link him to the crime."

As the magistrate closed the case, he had a few words for those who still remained in the courthouse.

"Man is given free will by God to do as he pleases, provided that free will is exercised responsibly for the good of the country to humankind in general. When greed and avarice take over, it is as if the devil has overcome your soul and your will to function normally and in the best interest of the country. If the Egyptians were to come to England and dig up the Westminster Abbey and remove the dead bodies of your kings and queens and smuggle them to Cairo, how would people of England react? You have removed the mummies from their graves, taken them to England for all to see, and kept them in your museums." His remarks addressed Sid Carter and James. "It is no defense to say that someone made me do this or that. It is in your power to control your actions. You have allowed the devil to enter you. Noble actions do keep the devil at bay. May God grant you wisdom to follow the right path."

He abruptly left the court and walked gingerly to his car. The ambassador and his entourage, who were in the courtroom, lost this case. Their influence with the judge obviously did not pay well. Disappointed that their best friends Sid Carter and Johnston had received ten years imprisonment, their only chance now was to appeal to the king for clemency. Little did they realize they only had less than twenty-four hours to make an appeal because the fate of the king hung in the balance.

11
The Nightingale Sings

My soul wants to fly away when
your presence calls it so sweetly
My soul wants to take flight,
when you whisper "Arise."
—Rumi

It was a perfect day. The sun blazed on the kingdom and a light breeze blew throughout the land as the king embarked on a peaceful walk through the palace grounds. His garden with its finely manicured lawns, perfectly trimmed hedges and weed free flower beds were a delight to his eyes. Every day, he leisurely strolled through his ornately designed landscapes and wondered how everything in the garden was so unblemished. He admired the bushes and their colorful flowers and noted how each bush's flower color matched the flowers on the adjacent bush. It was an impressive garden and therefore it took a little while for him to get from one end of the garden to the other.

At the far end of the garden was a pond and the hibiscus plants. Together with the rose and lilac bushes they formed an arc around the small body of water. Palm trees stood like sentries behind the bushes and provided shade. On most days a few birds enjoy the pond, splashing and chirping endlessly, socializing and finding relief from the blistering desert heat. They often sang as they hid amongst the boughs of foliage.

As the king ambled toward the pond, he noticed the crow and the duck were already there. The duck fluidly dove into the water while the crow poised himself on the edge of the pond. Suddenly a movement in the bushes caught the king's eye. A golden-brown rooster and a peacock emerged from behind the bushes and headed toward the pond. A thought came to him and he remembered a story that his mother told him when he was a child. His mother's sweet voice reverberated in his mind as the story unfolded:

"Once upon a time there was a man with three sons. The man was getting advanced in years and decided that he had struggled enough in life and it was time to hang up his boots. Though not despondent at having to retire, he reminded his three sons that it was now their turn to look after him. One day he called them all together to discuss their future.

"Now, you know I have never left this village in my life for anything. I have worked the leather and made boots out of them; I have attended to the horses and fitted iron shoes. I have been both a shoemaker and a blacksmith. Now that I am now growing in years, it is time for you three sons to make a living for yourselves. If any of you desire to take over the shoemaking business, you are most welcome to it. But I warn you, at the end of the day you will certainly starve."

The three sons declined taking over the business. Every morning the father would watch his three sons go off to the next village to find work and return that same evening with a day's wage. This went on for some time. The family was still poor, but happy. Then one day, all three sons returned home in the evening with much more than they had ever earned before.

"What did you get today, my eldest son?" asked the father of his eldest son.

"Today I dug the earth with my bare hands until they were sore. There, buried six feet deep, were nuggets of gold. I filled up my sack with all the gold I could lay my hands on. With my strength I ensured none came near the site. I fought off the old, the young, the poor, and the rich." His father's eyes glistened with flowing tears of joy.

"Oh, my son, you have made me proud!" Turning to his second son, the father addressed him: "Now, my second son, what did you bring for your father today?"

"I brought you a sack of plants. If chewed daily, it will give you eternal life—life that the pharaohs longed for but had eluded them."

"How wonderful! I could live forever, and the gold would come in handy," exclaimed the delighted father.

"Now, my third son, what did you bring for me today?" the father asked, turning to his youngest son.

"I have brought for you a sack full of the finest foods available anywhere, meant to be eaten only by the king. You will never stop eating once you have tasted what I have in this sack. I then went to the bar, got myself drunk, womanized a little, and at last made my way home."

As his father opened the sack, a rich aroma of spices available only from Hind and Mesopotamia emerged from the sack. He put his hand in the sack and brought out the best of rice, spices, and saffron. The fragrances enticed their senses and they all sat down to eat as the beggars gathered around them, jostling for a spot in the front row. But the beggars soon left disappointed, having not tasted even a morsel from the old man and his three sons.

"Now you see, my son," said the king's mother, "the four birds represent the attributes of the father and his three sons, namely greed, gluttony, lustfulness, and longing for eternal life. There is in every human being a dark side, which manifests itself through one's own willfulness or by the company one keeps. This company, a vile and corrupt lot, casts a dark shadow on one's soul, which ultimately ruins him to destitution. Read the signs in what you have just witnessed."

A cold shiver ran down the king's spine and beads of sweat trickled down his forehead as her warning lingered in his thoughts. It was an ominous sign, he thought. Rarely have all four birds come together in one place, and right in front of his eyes. He knew he was condemned, but he reasoned that perhaps it was not a bad omen. Perhaps it was simply a coincidence. He did not bear all attributes as exhibited by the four birds. He exhibited some, like gluttony, greed, and longing for eternal life. Then he thought to himself, it must be due the company he has kept—the ambassador and his ministers. Anxiety resurfaced as his hands shook at the thought of being destitute. Before he had time to compose himself, his imaginings were interrupted.

"Your Majesty, the ambassador and his party will be here shortly. You had planned to go duck hunting in Al-Fayum," the Minister of Culture reminded the king upon arriving at the palace. Now Al-Fayum had a large lake where thousands of ducks flocked every year on their journey south. Here the king and his ministers would go for leisure and mindless killing.

"I must have forgotten about it. Bring me my air gun, and ask Hakim to get my hunting clothes ready," commanded the king.

"Right away," said the minister as he ran into the palace to retrieve the gun and instruct the servant of the king's request. As the king walked into the palace from the garden, Hakim, his longtime servant, stood there waiting to speak to him.

"I have all these petitions from the peasants. They need your immediate attention. Will you look at them before you go hunting?" Hakim respectfully inquired.

"They can wait till I get back. I must not keep the ambassador waiting," declared the king as he quickly climbed up a set of stairs and disappeared down a short hallway. Within a few minutes he had changed into his hunting gear and was ready to go.

A black car pulled up to the palace gate and the sentry on duty opened the wrought iron gate to let the car through. Sitting in the backseat was a middle-aged English gentleman revealing a receding hairline.

"The king will soon join you," said the palace guard to the Englishman. The Englishman was none other than the British ambassador to Egypt. As the king stepped out of the palace into the waiting car, he was followed in another car by his ministers and businessmen, including Sid Carter of the Egyptian Date Company. On the way, the king and the ambassador engaged in idle conversation. The king related the story he was told as a child:

"Let me tell you a story of four birds: the crow, the peacock, the duck, and the rooster," the king began. "The crow was always the first to wake up each morning, as he liked to get the most out of the day. But he made a terrible ruckus with his crowing. None of the other birds could figure out what exactly he was crowing about. Nevertheless, he was the most unpopular bird around the palace. One day the crow walked over to the pond where the peacock, duck, and the rooster had gathered, who were already irritated by the crow's noise.

"'You seem to have lost your senses,' said the peacock. 'While everyone is asleep, you are the first to get up, making a terrible noise as if the whole world should be awake just because of you. You want to live for a thousand years, just like the pharaohs. Is that what the crown is all about?'

"'What are you complaining about?' retorted the crow to the peacock. 'You are so proud and arrogant, displaying all your bright and beautiful feathers and boasting how no one else has magnificent plumes.'

"The duck and the rooster, who kept out of the fray till now, joined in.

"'I must say, we all have our faults and our souls are darkened by faults,' injected the rooster.

"'Let us all eat from dawn to dusk. Eating tends to drown my sorrows. Try it and see for yourself whether it works for you or not,' said the duck, diving to the bottom of the pond and sticking his bill in the mud.

“There are some birds that live in paradise, like the nightingale, and there are others that infest the human soul and tear away at the core of that which is good and noble, destroying all hope of salvation for one’s soul. Now tell me, Mr. Ambassador, am I not in the company of people that are like the four birds?” asked the king.

“I don’t know what you mean,” the ambassador hastily replied.

“When your nation occupied my country, it boasted its superiority over us and fleeced it of its resources. You and Sid Carter are like the peacock and the duck, always proud, arrogant, and gluttonous. There are two ministers currently traveling with us and one of them, I believe, continuously frequents nightclubs and dancing bars, exhibiting lustful behavior. The other minister boasts about how he would keep company with the rich and the powerful, devoid of any principles. He wants to remain minister forever, whether the people approve of him or not,” said the king.

The ambassador was shocked with the king’s analogy. His face reddened, indicating a deep displeasure with the king, but he kept his remarks to himself. He figured he would get to the king at an appropriate time and place. He had rescued the king once before when his people were going to overthrow him and send him into exile.

Besides the four birds, there was Latifa, a subtle body that resided in each person, hidden by the *Rabb* with a veil. When the veil was lifted, certain historical events initiated by the Rabb were put into motion by the *Marbub* that no power on earth was capable of stopping. This was such a day when the *Rabb* lifted the veil of Latifa, and the king was in serious trouble. Meanwhile, in the vehicle transporting ministers and Sid Carter, it was business as usual.

"Our business will flourish and grow, provided we can keep the Egyptian masses in our control by limiting what we pay them. In this way, our resources can be channeled to the army so that they can control the masses in case of rioting," Sid plotted.

"My job as minister is to see that the masses do not accumulate wealth by keeping their wages low. This will keep our industries competitive with lots of cheap labor."

"If we both work together, we should be able to keep the workers where they belong—at the bottom, living day-to-day," said Sid mischievously. While they plotted the demise of the people, in the front car the ambassador had recovered from the earlier insult.

"The sun will never set on the British Empire. The other races are supposed to serve our royalty and therefore us. The taxes from the goods we sell go to the colonial office and are used to provide support to the local politicians, who are our friends," said the ambassador, taking a subtle jab at the king.

"Your support for me is much appreciated. The masses do not know that you are my friend, but they do not suspect anything ulterior in such a relationship," said the king.

Behind them the discussion continued. "We are your friends, Sid, even at the expense of our people. You provide us with the pay and pension, which we would never get if it were not for your government," said the Minister of Culture.

"And we appreciate your nightclubs and the women you bring along from your countries. It is hard to get good dancers here for the cabaret," the Minister of Local Government, now joining the conversation.

The king, though extravagant, was generally good to his people, providing basic services for the poor and the sick. But he was slowly being corrupted by the seedy lot of his entourage.

Upon reaching Al-Fayum, the party walked together debating the war and how the allies had been successful against the Germans. The different war tales of bravado and superior intelligence of the military quickly fanned from the king and the ambassador to the others in the party. On reaching the lakeshore, they noticed hundreds of birds chirping in the bushes.

"We will have a field day today," declared the king. "There are a hundred birds here. Take a shot and you are bound to bag a few, even if you are terrible at shooting!"

Then an inner voice interrupted the king's thinking.

Why must you shoot God's beautiful creatures? Isn't it a terrible waste? God creates and man destroys. Isn't this the whole story of the human race so far—mindless killing just for sport?

Then a voice from the dark recesses of the king's heart broke in, saying, *God will create more. Just go ahead and have fun—we all need fun in our lives.*

The benevolent voice was again heard. *How will you account for your deeds?*

This struggle between the voice of benevolence and that from the dark recesses of the king's soul continued for a little while, paralyzing the king's reason. Meanwhile the ambassador was bagging birds by the dozens.

"What? Lost your nerve?" asked the ambassador to the king. "Want to join the Salvation Army? There may be a place for you there, since they don't shoot anybody or anything, for that matter."

Someone sneezed, sending the birds scattering from the bushes. The king raised his rifle and gave the fleeing birds a few shots. Bang…bang… bang, went his rifle. Not a single shot caught any birds. Meanwhile, even the ministers were doing well in hunting ducks and were now competing with the ambassador for the most ducks hunted.

While they were hunting, in the church of Al-Fayum Reverend Wilson was conducting a service. Wearing an iron cross dangling from his neck by a thin cord, he put pieces of bread in wine, and repeated prayers over them, reminding the congregation of the miracle of Christ when he converted water to wine. The girl choir sang hymns while the reverend raised his goblet of wine in the air and drank from it. Soon the whole congregation participated in taking the blood and flesh of Christ.

Then the reverend did something strange that left the congregation gasping. He started to sing and plunged into a whirling dance like the Sufis of Cairo. He only stopped when he heard Latifa sing in her garden. Of course, his voice was no match for that of Latifa's.

Latifa was, of course, remembering the fateful day when her son was killed by a sentry bullet at Helwan. Her incorrigible sorrow was to last a lifetime. Her only regret that day was allowing her son to leave home late at night when there was always danger of someone getting shot at the military base. She had predicted a major event to happen this day, sometime later, which must have come to her in a dream, and the reverend was to play a major part in it.

The reverend came out of the church and stood at the front steps, observing Latifa attending to her rose garden and singing her heart out.

"Good morning, Latifa. How is your day so far?" said the reverend.

"Fair, fair. If only I could stop thinking about my son. It is hard after so many years," she said sadly.

"I know, my child, how tough it is to lose your only son. Have faith in God, and soon things will get better."

"Today I will sing my heart out and Mustapha expects you to join in a special ceremony. It is to mark the end of a chapter in the life of this country. If I don't see you, take good care of yourself. We will meet in a better place." The reverend did not understand, nor did he hear the words "better place."

"I will go to Cairo as soon as I have finished here," he answered as he entered the church to finish off the ceremonies. The congregation was in tears, anticipating great events to unfold that day. Reverend Wilson finished his sermon with the following words:

"I am leaving today to go to Cairo, because our Father in heaven has ordained that for me. When I am there, I will undertake a journey to the far corners of heaven, and ask Father to show reprieve to this land by banishing the evil of occupation and corruption." Then his tone changed to a gentler, more thoughtful one. "If I decided to stay, you can be assured of my constant watch over you that you may refrain from evil and follow the path of truth and gentleness."

A pool of saliva accumulated in his mouth and he swallowed hard. The congregation grew worried that the reverend might pass out any minute. Some rushed frantically to the stage to ensure he was all right, and others opened the church doors to let in fresh air. A slight breeze blowing earlier was now brewing to be a full-fledged storm. The church door slammed with the force of the wind, the people screamed in panic, and Reverend Wilson took leave and went to the rear where he sat down on a chair brought by a parishioner There was speculation going on among the members that their priest was ill with a mental disease, since he had never spoken to them about such matters, as well with such grimness. Some said he saw the light of Christ, and that Mary, Christ's mother, had come to get him.

Meanwhile the king and his party were having the time of their lives picnicking, hunting, and swimming in the lake. Bags full of ducks lay nearby, the finest tablecloths lined endless rows of picnic tables on the lake, wine flowed freely, and laughter saw no end.

The four birds in the palace garden had now scattered and menacing clouds gathered above, and an ominous darkness enveloped the garden.

Mustapha arrived in Cairo and went straight to the tekke. Here a special dance called the *mukabele* was about to begin. Like all dances, Mustapha took the ritual bow from the other *Mevlevis*, and the spinning began.

At the same time, across the city the army was preparing advances against the king. Tanks began to roll in from their bases and Captain Hasan, who was arrested by the British for espionage, was in charge.

The king was on his way from Al-Fayum to Cairo. On his way, he stopped at the pyramids at Giza, where a flat tire on his limousine forced him off the road. Someone told him that his life would be in danger if he went to Cairo. The delay, presumably a divine intervention, had enabled the army to set in motion the plan to take over the palace before the king had a chance to order reinforcements from his loyal troops.

As the circle of the *Mevlevis* began to form, so did the tanks surrounding the palace. It was as if the tank commander was actually present in the *tekke* and taking part in the ceremony. Although Hassan was absent from the *mukabele*, the reverend had left an empty spot next to him.

Having surrounded the palace, Hasan decided to wait it out until the *mukabele* inside the tekke was over before he entered the palace grounds to arrest the king. At best, the punishment would be banishment from Egypt. The king was further delayed at Giza, not only from a flat tire on his car but a fierce sandstorm that was making its way from the north.

The *mukabele* being over, Hasan proceeded to enter the palace grounds. He was stopped at the gates by armed guards.

"I have come to see the king," said Hasan fiercely.

"The king has gone hunting and won't be back till the evening," said one of the guards.

"Then I have come to take over the palace. I possess authority from the army commander, who is also your boss,

Major General Gamel. So, obey his orders and let me in or we will use force."

The guards discussed the options available with each other and decided not to let Hasan in. There were shots fired, and one of the guards got hit in the stomach. The other guard, having two hundred soldiers outside the gate, was still no match for such an overwhelming force; he surrendered and let Hassan enter the palace grounds. The gates flung open as Hasan marched in with half a dozen men. The rest of the men in tanks took position outside the palace grounds. After about three hours, the king had not yet arrived. He had gone straight to Alexandria. Meanwhile in Alexandria, tanks had also rolled and occupied the outside of the palace.

"I have come to claim my palace for the people who have me as their king," demanded the king as he tried to negotiate with the palace guards.

"You have no palace. Today you are jobless. The only place for you is exile, where you shall be totally cut off from your people, whose trust you have violated by your association with the thieves and looters of this country. You are a disgrace to your people," said an angry guard, now flushed and sweating profusely.

The king was made to collect his belongings and taken to a waiting yacht to go into exile.

The *kanun*, the *ut,* and the *tambur* had fallen silent, being laid to rest in their cases. The Mevlevis had left the tekke. Mustapha and the reverend strolled together toward the garden to sit on a wooden bench.

"The story of the king losing his throne—is that of mankind itself? The highest creation on earth, mankind, is 'king' himself. When man does things on this earth that are against the divine will, he will lose his 'palace.' He will lose his special status with God and will no longer be protected by his light. He will be forced into exile where he will remain devoid of all wisdom and knowledge. Until he begins to stay on the 'course' prescribed for him, he will be forbidden to reclaim his noble status."

"That's most interesting," observed the reverend.

"You were spurred from your little cozy English world of Sunday service and visiting old ladies to become an agent of God—to take on our king and the mighty British Empire, to begin to dismantle it because it had become an eyesore on the values of the human landscape."

"And why would I be chosen when there existed others who could have excelled at the task with their knowledge of warfare?" the reverend wondered.

"Because it had to be peaceful, since violence is a hindrance toward our journey to eternity. You were of a peaceful nature—an attribute of rare quality."

Mustapha looked around and saw Marju on the garden wall. Marju stared at him and Mustapha stared back. "He doesn't want me to go further," said Mustapha, pointing to Marju.

During the *mukabele*, the reverend had unknowingly put both his hands skyward—an intense form of supplication. It made it possible for his prayers to be answered. Mustapha did not want to relate this incident to John, since it was rare and only used for change of momentous proportions; a historical event. It was Latifa who initiated this gesture by raising her hands skywards, while the reverend simultaneously followed the gesture.

The reverend was in fact a vehicle for the transmission of Latifa's supplication.

"But I will explain only a small part to you, since it is important for you to understand," said Mustapha.

Though the reverend had acclimated to the hot and humid weather, beads of sweat popped up along the crease in his forehead, which he wiped with a handkerchief. Mustapha was also sweating, but he did not attempt to wipe the sweat off his brow. Mustapha continued:

"At the beginning, in your struggle with everyday life, a path was created for you with a destination in mind. You did not know where this path would lead you to, or how soon it would come to an end."

"What was the significance of this path?"

Mustapha explained, "It was a course set for you without your input into it so that you may do something extraordinary—something that is not given to every individual." Mustapha gazed straight ahead in a southerly direction, as if his words were coming from the distant pyramids.

"What is in store for me next?" asked the reverend.

"You still have a few 'rivers' to cross before you set sail for the sea of eternity," said Mustapha.

"What will I find when I reach the sea?" asked the reverend.

"Here your 'raft' will be joined by many others, all similar and all sailing ultimately into the divine sunset where the raft and the sun are indistinguishable from each other, the raft having merged into the sun. As the divine text says: 'From whom we have come and to whom we shall return.'"

Immediately after he said it, Mustapha slumped over, fell off the bench, and hit his head on the floor. A two-inch gash developed on his forehead, blood oozing from it. The reverend sat there as if shell-shocked. He took out his handkerchief and applied it firmly to the forehead wound. But Mustapha was gone. John calmly made his way inside the tekke. He knew it was pointless to summon help. He found a dervish in the change room, and together they carried the body inside and wrapped it in a simple white cotton cloth and laid it down on the same spot he used to occupy when conducting mukabele. After paying their respects, the rest of the dervishes put his body in a simple wooden coffin and carried it to a waiting donkey cart. Before the cart left, the reverend had put a red rose on top of the coffin. The word had spread fast that Mustapha had passed away. A crowd of well-wishers lined the road from the tekke to the cemetery. He was buried at sunset on July 23rd, 1952.

"When the rose is gone and the garden faded
You will no longer hear the nightingale's song
The beloved is all; the lover just a veil
The beloved is living; the lover a dead thing
If love withholds its strengthening care,
The lover is left like a bird without care,
The lover is left like a bird without wings.
How will I be awake and be aware,
If the light of the beloved is absent.
Love wills that this word be brought forth." – Rumi

The lover of the divine and divine were now one. The king was sent into exile, the British army left soon after, and a sad chapter of history for the people of Egypt was now closed.

The subsequent day, Reverend John made his way to the airport to take the next and final flight to London. This passage in the life of John Wilson comes to an end and another one to begin somewhere else.

The End